俠盜 羅賓漢

原著 *Howard Pyle*

改編 **Anne Suzane**

Robin Hood

Contents
目　錄

羅賓漢淪爲盜賊
HOW ROBIN HOOD BECAME AN OUTLAW
1

羅賓漢結識短腳約翰
HOW ROBIN HOOD MET LITTLE JOHN
17

羅賓漢變身屠夫，和州長共進晚餐
HOW ROBIN HOOD BECAME BUTCHER, AND ATE DINNER AT THE SHERIFF'S CASTLE
21

短腳約翰爲州長做事的來龍去脈
HOW LITTLE JOHN STARTED TO WORK FOR THE SHERIFF
27

州長的三個能幹僕人失蹤後再現
HOW THE SHERIFF LOST THREE GOOD SERVANTS AND FOUND THEM AGAIN
31

俠盜　羅賓漢

羅賓漢結識血腥威爾
HOW ROBIN HOOD MET WILL SCARLET
37

羅賓漢找尋塔克修道士
ROBIN GOES TO FIND FRIAR TUCK
41

羅賓漢安排婚禮
ROBIN ARRANGES A MARRIAGE
47

羅賓漢的三名手下被抓和被救的過程
THREE MEN ARE CAPTURED AND RESCUED
51

乞丐智勝羅賓漢
ROBIN IS OUTWITTED BY A BEGGAR
55

吉斯本的凱依與羅賓漢纏鬥，
羅賓漢救出短腳約翰
ROBIN MEETS GUY OF GISBANE AND RESCUES LITTLE JOHN
59

瑪莉安和羅賓漢重逢
MARION AND ROBIN MEET AGAIN
65

Robin Hood

射箭比賽
THE ARCHERY COMPETITION
69

羅賓漢和補鍋匠
ROBIN AND THE TINKER
75

製革匠遇見羅賓漢和短腳約翰
THE TANNER MEETS ROBIN AND LITTLE JOHN
81

理察爵士和瑪莉安的駕臨
SIR RICHARD AND MARION ARRIVE
87

曦拂主教的造訪
THE BISHOP OF HEREFORD PAYS A VISIT
93

曦拂主教搜尋羅賓漢
THE BISHOP OF HEREFORD LOOKS FOR ROBIN
97

俠盜 羅賓漢

州長舉辦另一場射箭比賽
THE SHERIFF HOLDS ANOTHER ARCHERY COMPETITION
101

拯救威爾・史都特利的行動
THE RESCUE OF WILL STUTELY
107

李理察為羅賓漢舉行慶功宴
RICHARD OF LEA AND ROBIN HOOD CELEBRATE
113

一位爵士出現在雪霧森林
A KNIGHT APPEARS IN SHERWOOD FOREST
119

羅賓漢和瑪莉安結為夫婦
ROBIN HOOD AND MAID MARION GET MARRIED
125

羅賓漢與死神交戰
HOW ROBIN HOOD MET HIS DEATH
131

Robin Hood

HOW ROBIN HOOD BECAME AN OUTLAW

This story begins This story begins when Harold II was King of England. At this time there were certain forests in the North of England where only King Harold could hunt animals. One of the most important was near Nottingham. It was called Sherwood Forest. The head forester was called Hugh Fitzooth and his son, Robin.

Robin was born in 1160. When he was young, Robin learned to use a bow and arrow. He also loved to hear his father tell stories of famous outlaws. Robin's best friends were Will Gamewell, son of Hugh Fitzooth's brother, and Marion Fitzwalter.

俠盜 羅賓漢

羅賓漢淪爲盜賊

故事開始於哈洛三世在位爲英國國王。這時期英國北方有一些森林，只有哈洛國王可以在裡面打獵。其中最重要的一個鄰近那汀罕。它被稱爲雪霧森林。國王手下帶領打獵的龍頭爲休'費左斯和其子羅賓漢。

羅賓漢生於 1160 年。他從小就開始學習使用弓箭。他也愛聽父親敘述有名的盜匪傳說。羅賓漢最要好的朋友是威兒'蓋蔚爾，他叔叔的兒子，和瑪莉安'費華特。

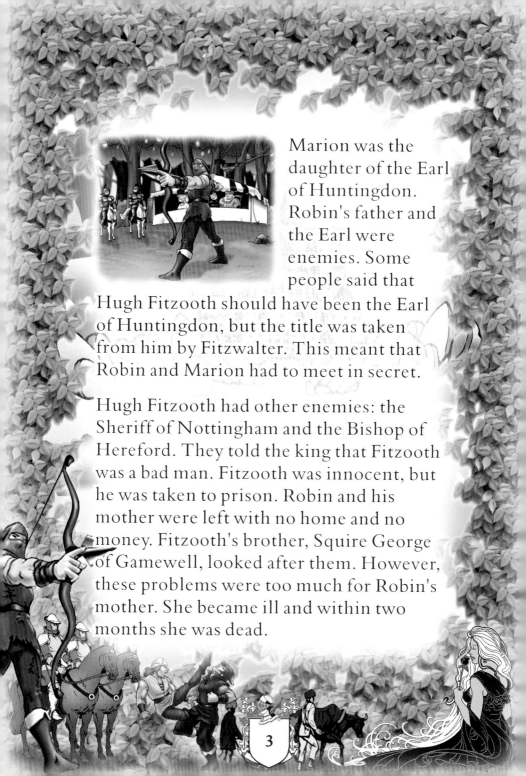

Marion was the daughter of the Earl of Huntingdon. Robin's father and the Earl were enemies. Some people said that Hugh Fitzooth should have been the Earl of Huntingdon, but the title was taken from him by Fitzwalter. This meant that Robin and Marion had to meet in secret.

Hugh Fitzooth had other enemies: the Sheriff of Nottingham and the Bishop of Hereford. They told the king that Fitzooth was a bad man. Fitzooth was innocent, but he was taken to prison. Robin and his mother were left with no home and no money. Fitzooth's brother, Squire George of Gamewell, looked after them. However, these problems were too much for Robin's mother. She became ill and within two months she was dead.

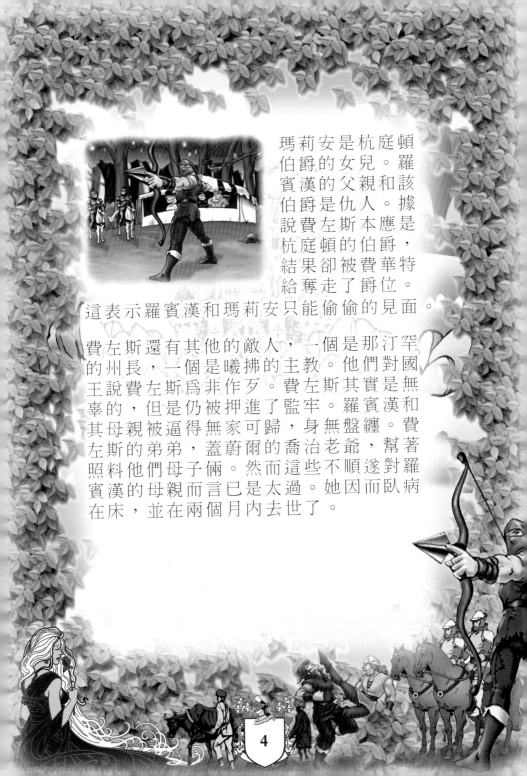

瑪莉安是杭庭頓伯爵的女兒。羅賓漢的父親和該伯爵是仇人。據說費左斯本應是杭庭頓的伯爵，結果卻被費華特給奪走了爵位。這表示羅賓漢和瑪莉安只能偷偷的見面。

費左斯還有其他的敵人，一個是那汀罕的州長，一個是曦拂的主教。他們對國王說費左斯爲非作歹。費左斯其實是無辜的，但是仍被押進了監牢。羅賓漢和其母親被逼得無家可歸，身無盤纏。費左斯的弟弟，蓋蔚爾的喬治老爺，幫著照料他們母子倆。然而這些不順遂對羅賓漢的母親而言已是太過。她因而臥病在床，並在兩個月內去世了。

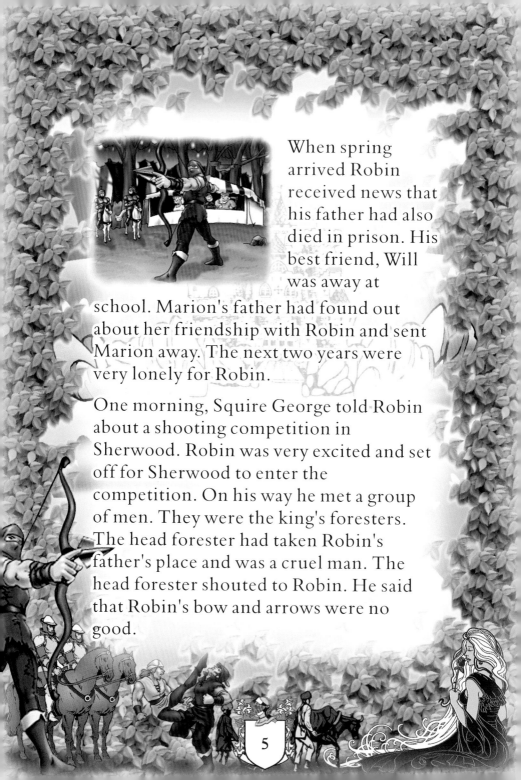

When spring arrived Robin received news that his father had also died in prison. His best friend, Will was away at school. Marion's father had found out about her friendship with Robin and sent Marion away. The next two years were very lonely for Robin.

One morning, Squire George told Robin about a shooting competition in Sherwood. Robin was very excited and set off for Sherwood to enter the competition. On his way he met a group of men. They were the king's foresters. The head forester had taken Robin's father's place and was a cruel man. The head forester shouted to Robin. He said that Robin's bow and arrows were no good.

春天來的時候，羅賓漢聞訊父親也已死在牢內。而他的好友威兒則在外求學。瑪莉安的父親發現他們之間有來往時，也把瑪莉安送走了。羅賓漢在接下來的兩個年頭過得很孤寂。

一天早晨，喬治老爺告訴羅賓漢，即將有場射箭比賽在雪霧森林舉行。羅賓漢聽了很興奮，於是起身前往雪霧森林，準備加入比賽。途中他遇上一群人。他們是國王的狩獵人馬。他們的領導者取代了羅賓漢父親的位子，他是一個殘暴的人。那狩獵隊長對羅賓漢吆喝。他說羅賓漢的弓箭不利。

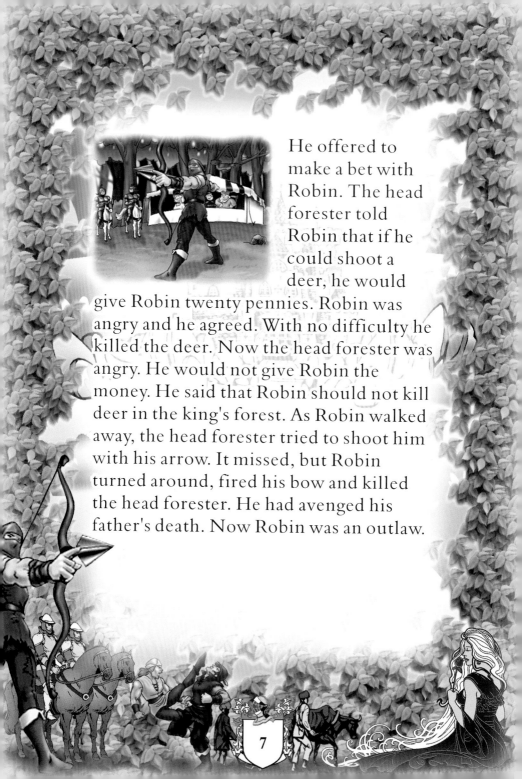

He offered to make a bet with Robin. The head forester told Robin that if he could shoot a deer, he would give Robin twenty pennies. Robin was angry and he agreed. With no difficulty he killed the deer. Now the head forester was angry. He would not give Robin the money. He said that Robin should not kill deer in the king's forest. As Robin walked away, the head forester tried to shoot him with his arrow. It missed, but Robin turned around, fired his bow and killed the head forester. He had avenged his father's death. Now Robin was an outlaw.

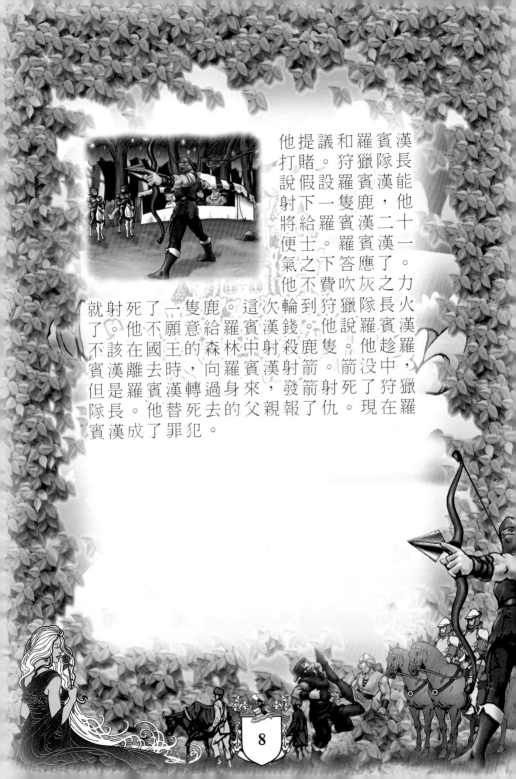

他提議和羅賓漢打賭。狩獵隊長說假設羅賓漢能射下一隻鹿，他將給羅賓漢二十便士。羅賓漢一氣之下答應了。

他不費吹灰之力就射死了一隻鹿。這次輪到狩獵隊長火了。他不願意給羅賓漢錢。他說羅賓漢不該在國王的森林中射殺鹿隻。他趁羅賓漢離去時，向羅賓漢射箭。箭没中，但是羅賓漢轉過身來，發箭射死了狩獵隊長。他替死去的父親報了仇。現在羅賓漢成了罪犯。

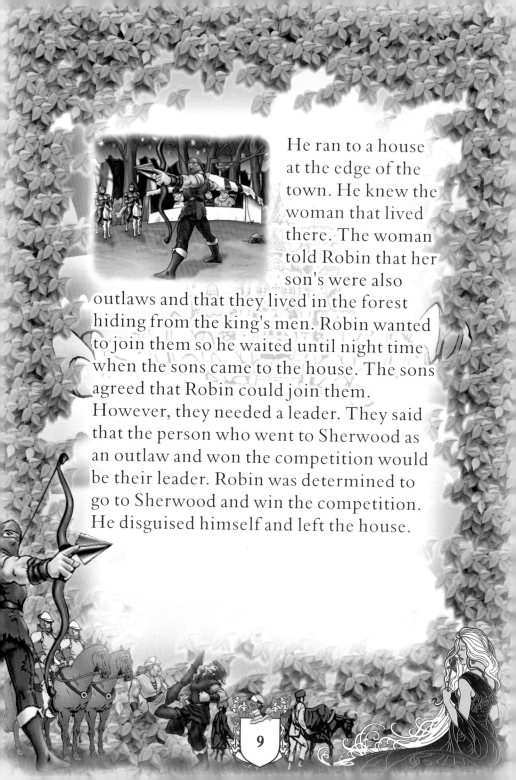

He ran to a house at the edge of the town. He knew the woman that lived there. The woman told Robin that her son's were also outlaws and that they lived in the forest hiding from the king's men. Robin wanted to join them so he waited until night time when the sons came to the house. The sons agreed that Robin could join them. However, they needed a leader. They said that the person who went to Sherwood as an outlaw and won the competition would be their leader. Robin was determined to go to Sherwood and win the competition. He disguised himself and left the house.

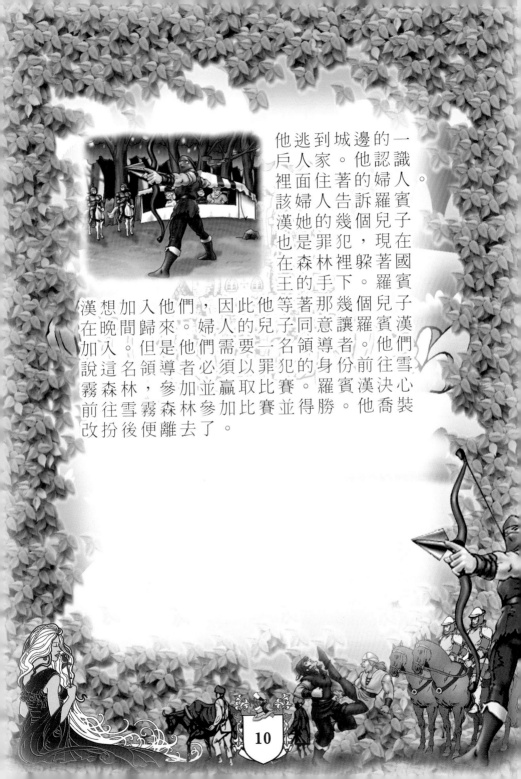

他逃到城邊的一戶人家。他認識裡面住著的婦人。該婦人告訴羅賓漢她的幾個兒子也是罪犯，現在在森林裡躲著國王的手下。羅賓漢想加入他們，因此他等著那幾個兒子在晚間歸來。婦人的兒子同意讓羅賓漢加入。但是他們需要一名領導者。他們說這名領導者必須以罪犯的身份前往雪霧森林，參加並贏取比賽。羅賓漢決心前往雪霧森林參加比賽並得勝。他喬裝改扮後便離去了。

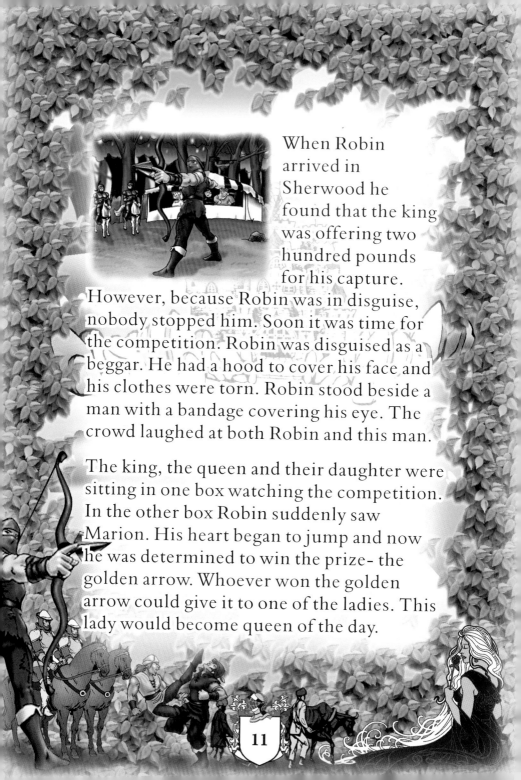

When Robin arrived in Sherwood he found that the king was offering two hundred pounds for his capture. However, because Robin was in disguise, nobody stopped him. Soon it was time for the competition. Robin was disguised as a beggar. He had a hood to cover his face and his clothes were torn. Robin stood beside a man with a bandage covering his eye. The crowd laughed at both Robin and this man.

The king, the queen and their daughter were sitting in one box watching the competition. In the other box Robin suddenly saw Marion. His heart began to jump and now he was determined to win the prize- the golden arrow. Whoever won the golden arrow could give it to one of the ladies. This lady would become queen of the day.

羅賓漢抵達雪霧森林時，發現國王下令以二百塊金幣緝拿他。但由於羅賓漢已經改裝，沒人阻攔他。不久比賽開始。羅賓漢現在看起來像個乞丐。他用連身帽蓋住臉，身上的衣服破破爛爛。他站在一個戴著眼罩的獨眼龍旁邊。其他人都嘲笑他和羅賓漢。

國王，皇后和他們的女兒都坐在包廂內觀看比賽。在另一個包廂內羅賓漢瞧見了瑪莉安。他的心撲撲的跳了起來，現在他暗下決心一定要拿到獎品一金弓。拿到金弓的人可以把它獻給在場的一位女士。該女士將是當日的皇后。

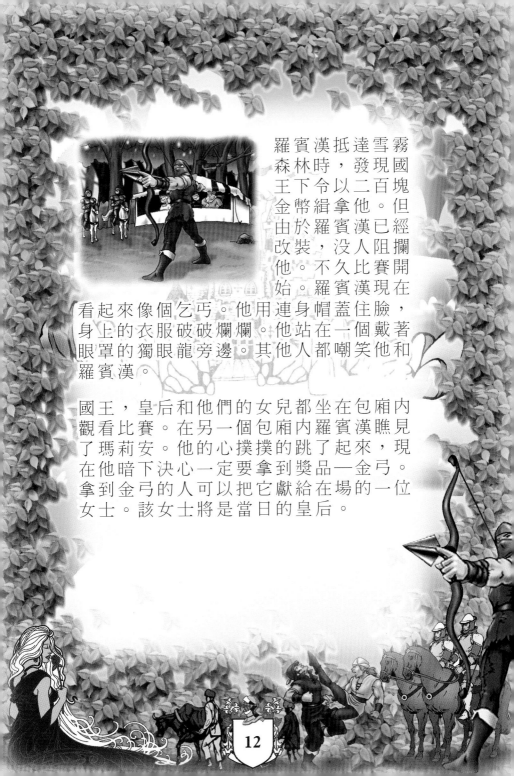

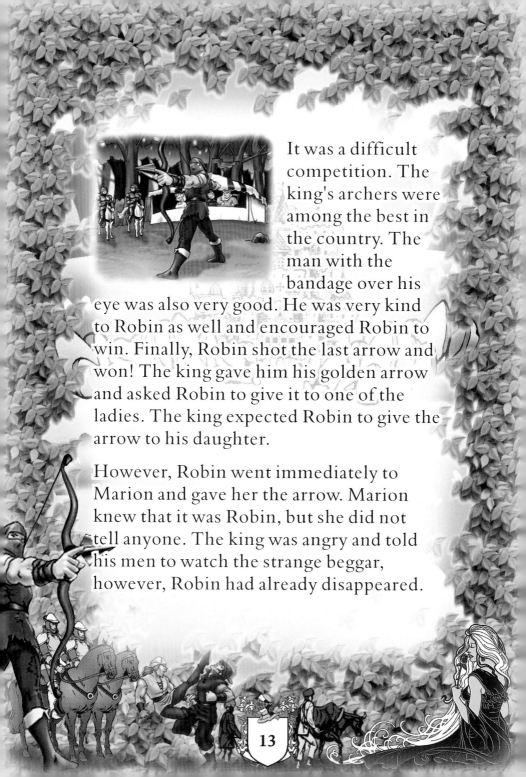

It was a difficult competition. The king's archers were among the best in the country. The man with the bandage over his eye was also very good. He was very kind to Robin as well and encouraged Robin to win. Finally, Robin shot the last arrow and won! The king gave him his golden arrow and asked Robin to give it to one of the ladies. The king expected Robin to give the arrow to his daughter.

However, Robin went immediately to Marion and gave her the arrow. Marion knew that it was Robin, but she did not tell anyone. The king was angry and told his men to watch the strange beggar, however, Robin had already disappeared.

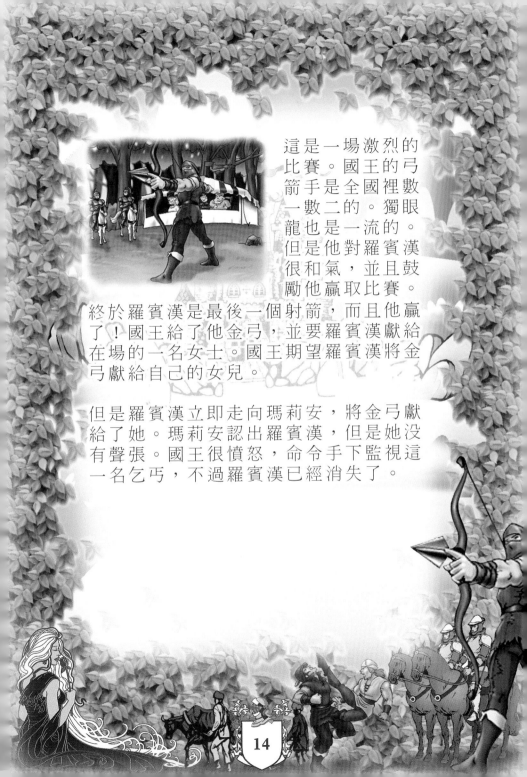

這是一場激烈的比賽。國王的弓箭手是全國裡數一數二的。獨眼龍也是一流的。但是他對羅賓漢很和氣，並且鼓勵他贏取比賽。

終於羅賓漢是最後一個射箭，而且他贏了！國王給了他金弓，並要羅賓漢獻給在場的一名女士。國王期望羅賓漢將金弓獻給自己的女兒。

但是羅賓漢立即走向瑪莉安，將金弓獻給了她。瑪莉安認出羅賓漢，但是她沒有聲張。國王很憤怒，命令手下監視這一名乞丐，不過羅賓漢已經消失了。

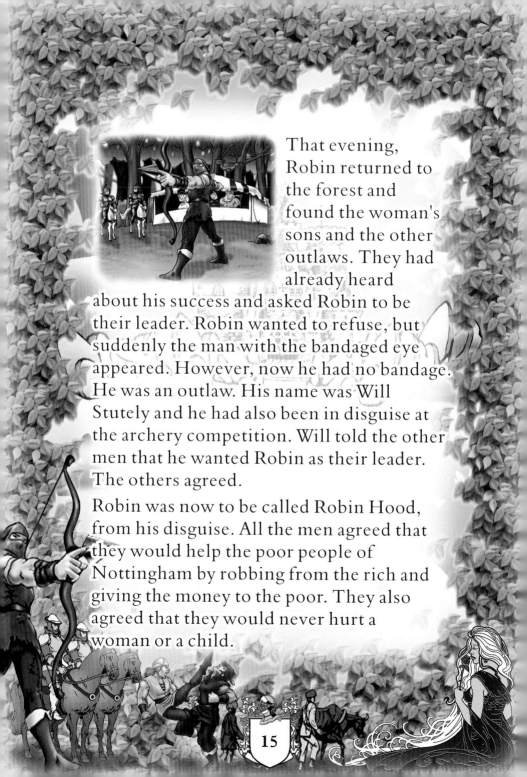

That evening, Robin returned to the forest and found the woman's sons and the other outlaws. They had already heard about his success and asked Robin to be their leader. Robin wanted to refuse, but suddenly the man with the bandaged eye appeared. However, now he had no bandage. He was an outlaw. His name was Will Stutely and he had also been in disguise at the archery competition. Will told the other men that he wanted Robin as their leader. The others agreed.

Robin was now to be called Robin Hood, from his disguise. All the men agreed that they would help the poor people of Nottingham by robbing from the rich and giving the money to the poor. They also agreed that they would never hurt a woman or a child.

當晚羅賓漢回到森林，找到婦人的兒子和其他的罪犯。這些人早已聽說羅賓漢得勝的消息，於是要求羅賓漢當他們的領導者。羅賓漢正想拒絕，突然獨眼龍出現了。只是這次他沒戴著眼罩。他是一名罪犯。他叫威爾'史塔利，也是爲了射箭比賽而改裝。威爾向衆人表示他希望羅賓漢來領導他們。其他人都同意了。

羅賓漢由於他的喬裝現被稱爲羅賓漢。所有人都異口同聲表示要劫富濟貧，來幫助那汀罕的窮人。他們也都同意絕不去傷害婦女和小孩。

HOW ROBIN HOOD MET LITTLE JOHN

Robin Hood and his men continued to take money and expensive goods from the rich travelers who passed through the forest. They gave all of this to the poor. Soon they were very popular among the local villagers and many joined the group. Before long, Robin's followers grew to around eighty men.

One summer's day, Robin went in search of adventure. As he was crossing the small footbridge over the river he met a tall stranger. The bridge was too small for both men to pass. However, neither man would move. They started to fight with sticks until the stranger hit Robin hard on the head. Robin fell into the river.

羅賓漢結識短腳約翰

羅賓漢及其手下陸續對穿梭於森林中的富有過客搶劫錢財和貴重物品。他們將所得來的東西全部施與窮人。他們旋即受到當地村民的歡迎，並有更多人加入他們的行列。不久羅賓漢的手下就增加到八十人左右。

某個夏日，羅賓漢外出探險。來到河上的一座小橋中間時，他和一個高大的陌生人迎面對上。這座橋太小，無法讓兩個人同時通過。但是這兩人也都互不退讓。他們開始用手杖打起來，最後陌生人在羅賓漢的頭上重擊了一下。羅賓漢落水。

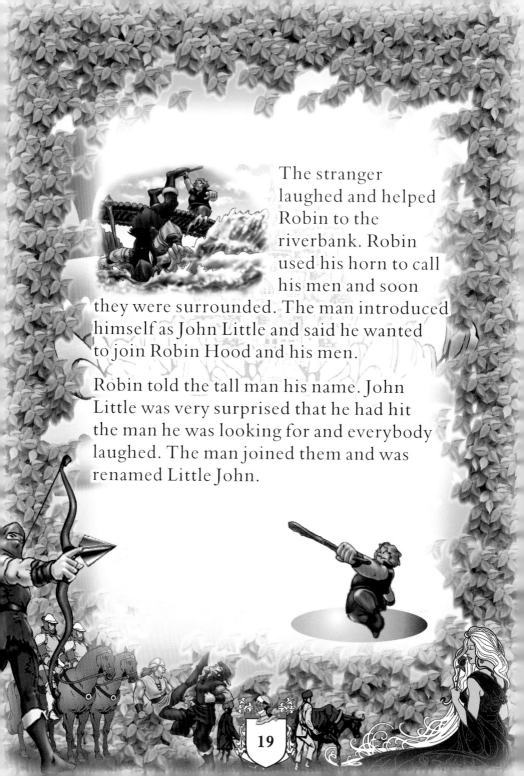

The stranger laughed and helped Robin to the riverbank. Robin used his horn to call his men and soon they were surrounded. The man introduced himself as John Little and said he wanted to join Robin Hood and his men.

Robin told the tall man his name. John Little was very surprised that he had hit the man he was looking for and everybody laughed. The man joined them and was renamed Little John.

陌生人大笑，同時將羅賓漢救到河岸邊。羅賓漢用號角呼叫他的手下出來，不久衆人就將他們兩人團團圍住。這人自稱是約翰'立地，他表示想加入羅賓漢的陣營中。

羅賓漢向這個人高馬大的約翰自我介紹。約翰很訝異這個被他修理的人竟然就是他要找的羅賓漢，衆人爲此哈哈大笑。這人加入他們，並被改名爲短腳約翰。

HOW ROBIN HOOD BECAME BUTCHER, AND ATE DINNER AT THE SHERIFF'S CASTLE

The following day a group of Robin's men were fired upon by the king's men as they tried to kill a deer. Robin's men fired back and the king's men ran away. They told the king what had happened and he was very angry. He was determined to catch Robin Hood.

A few days after this Little John disappeared. Robin was worried because he thought the king might have taken him. Immediately Robin went to Nottingham to find out what had happened. He asked his men to stay at the edge of the forest in case he needed their help.

羅賓漢變身屠夫，和州長共進晚餐

隔天羅賓漢手下的一群人正要捕殺一隻鹿時遭到國王的人馬開槍。羅賓漢的人還手，國王的人馬逃之夭夭。他們回去稟告國王這件事，國王聽了很震怒。他決心定要捉拿住羅賓漢。

幾天之後短腳約翰不見了蹤影。羅賓漢覺得擔心，因爲他想國王可能把他給抓走了。羅賓漢立即動身到那汀罕去探查。他要手下佈署在森林的周圍，好隨時給與他支援。

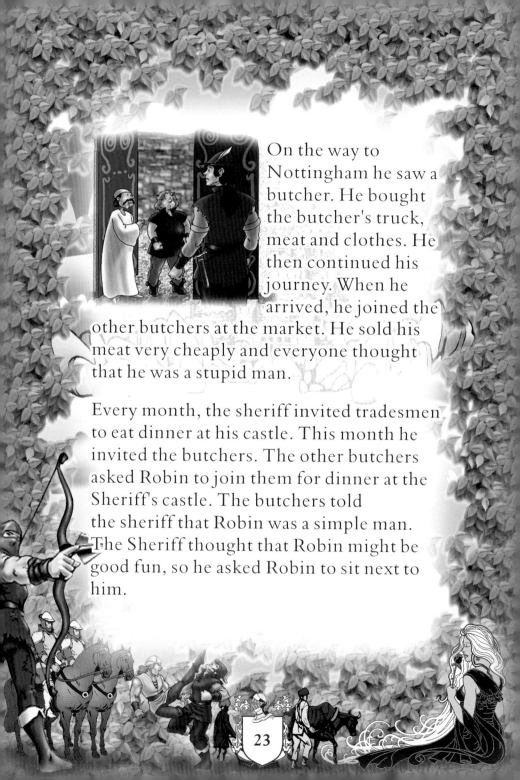

On the way to Nottingham he saw a butcher. He bought the butcher's truck, meat and clothes. He then continued his journey. When he arrived, he joined the other butchers at the market. He sold his meat very cheaply and everyone thought that he was a stupid man.

Every month, the sheriff invited tradesmen to eat dinner at his castle. This month he invited the butchers. The other butchers asked Robin to join them for dinner at the Sheriff's castle. The butchers told the sheriff that Robin was a simple man. The Sheriff thought that Robin might be good fun, so he asked Robin to sit next to him.

在到那汀罕的途中他遇見一個屠夫。他把屠夫的車子、肉品、衣服全部給買下來。然後他繼續他的旅程。到了城裡，羅賓漢混入市場內其他屠夫的行列。他將肉便宜的賣出，每個人都認爲他是個笨蛋。

每個月州長都會邀請生意人到他的城堡裡用餐。這個月他邀請的是屠夫。所有的屠夫都要羅賓漢和他們一起到州長的城堡內吃大餐。屠夫們告訴州長羅賓漢是個頭腦簡單的人。州長心想或許他可以好好來捉弄羅賓漢一下，所以要羅賓漢坐在他旁邊。

Robin told the sheriff that he had many horses to sell. The sheriff was a greedy man and so he wanted to buy them. He offered a very low price because he believed Robin was stupid. Robin agreed to go with the sheriff to see the horses the following day.

At that moment the door opened and a servant entered. It was Little John! Robin was very shocked to see him. He thought that John had betrayed him. However, John quietly told Robin to meet him in the kitchen that evening.

羅賓漢告訴州長說自己有很多馬匹要兜售。州長是個貪婪的人，便要買下那些馬匹。他出了很低的價錢，因爲他相信羅賓漢很蠢。羅賓漢答應隔天陪同州長去看馬。

此時一個僕人推了門進來。是短腳約翰！羅賓漢看到他很震驚。他以爲約翰背叛了他。但是約翰悄悄的叫羅賓漢當晚在廚房和他見面。

HOW LITTLE JOHN STARTED TO WORK FOR THE SHERIFF

A few days before the butchers' dinner, there had been a fair at the sheriff's castle. At the fair was a man named Eric of Lincoln. He was famous throughout the county for being a mean man. On this day he challenged many people to a fight. Eric always won.

After defeating many people, Eric saw a beggar. The beggar was laughing at him.

Eric challenged the beggar to a fight. After a long battle, the beggar finally hit Eric with his stick and knocked him to the ground. The beggar had won. After this, the beggar entered the shooting competition. He was so good that the sheriff asked him to work at the castle. The beggar agreed.

短腳約翰爲州長做事的來龍去脈

在這場餐會之前的幾天，州長的城堡裡舉行著一個園遊會。當時有個來自林肯的艾瑞克。他的壞心眼舉國皆知。這一天他向許多人挑戰對打。艾瑞克總是贏。

在打敗許多人之後，艾瑞克看到一名乞丐。乞丐正在嘲笑他。

艾瑞克便向那名乞丐挑戰。纏鬥許久之後，乞丐終於用拐杖將艾瑞克擊倒在地。乞丐獲勝。在此之後，乞丐進入射箭比賽。由於他的技術高超，州長要他留在城堡裡工作。乞丐答應了。

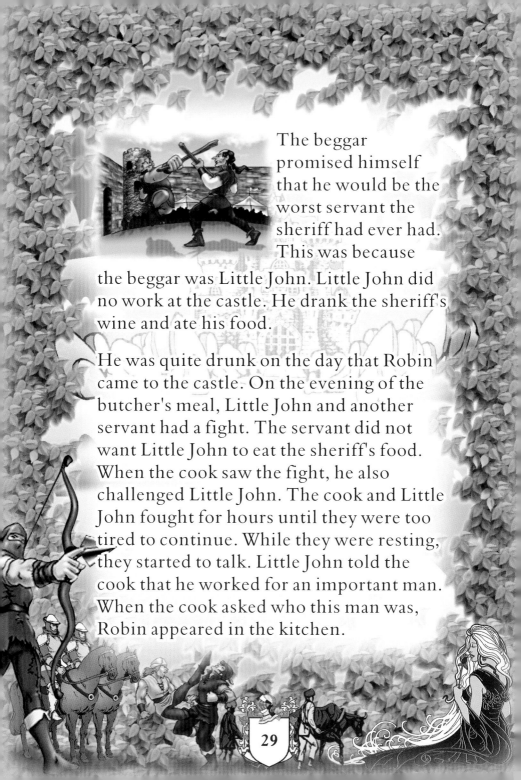

The beggar promised himself that he would be the worst servant the sheriff had ever had. This was because the beggar was Little John. Little John did no work at the castle. He drank the sheriff's wine and ate his food.

He was quite drunk on the day that Robin came to the castle. On the evening of the butcher's meal, Little John and another servant had a fight. The servant did not want Little John to eat the sheriff's food. When the cook saw the fight, he also challenged Little John. The cook and Little John fought for hours until they were too tired to continue. While they were resting, they started to talk. Little John told the cook that he worked for an important man. When the cook asked who this man was, Robin appeared in the kitchen.

乞丐暗下決心要當一個州長所見過的最糟糕的僕人。因爲這個乞丐就是短腳約翰。短腳約翰在城堡裡根本不做事。他喝州長的酒，吃州長的食物。

羅賓漢來城堡的那天，他喝得醉醺醺的。屠夫們來用餐的那一晚，短腳約翰和另一名僕人打了一架。該名僕人不讓短腳約翰吃州長的食物。廚師看到他們在打架時，也向短腳約翰挑戰。廚師和短腳約翰打了數個小時，最後兩人都累到無法再繼續。他們在休息時聊了起來。短腳約翰告訴廚師他爲一個重要人物工作。廚師問這重要人物是誰時，羅賓漢正好出現在廚房。

How The Sheriff Lost Three Good Servants And Found Them Again

The cook was amazed to meet Robin Hood. He asked if he could join his men and Robin agreed. The cook and Little John took all the silver and the food from the sheriff's kitchen and went to join the other men in Sherwood forest.

The next day, Robin and the sheriff went into the woods to see the horses. Robin told the sheriff that he was scared of Robin Hood. The sheriff said he was not. Soon they came across a large herd of the king's deer. Robin told the sheriff that these deer were his horses. Robin then blew his horn and all his men appeared. The sheriff was very surprised and very worried.

州長的三個能幹僕人失蹤後再現

廚師見到羅賓漢很訝異。他向羅賓漢請求加入他的人馬，羅賓漢同意了。廚師和短腳約翰於是從州長的廚房取走所有的銀器以及食物，然後到雪霧森林和其他人碰面。

第二天，羅賓漢陪同州長到森林中檢視馬匹。他告訴州長他很畏懼羅賓漢。州長說他不怕。不久他們遇見國王擁有的一大群鹿。羅賓漢說這些鹿就是他的馬。然後羅賓漢吹號角，他的手下出現了。州長感到既驚又憂。

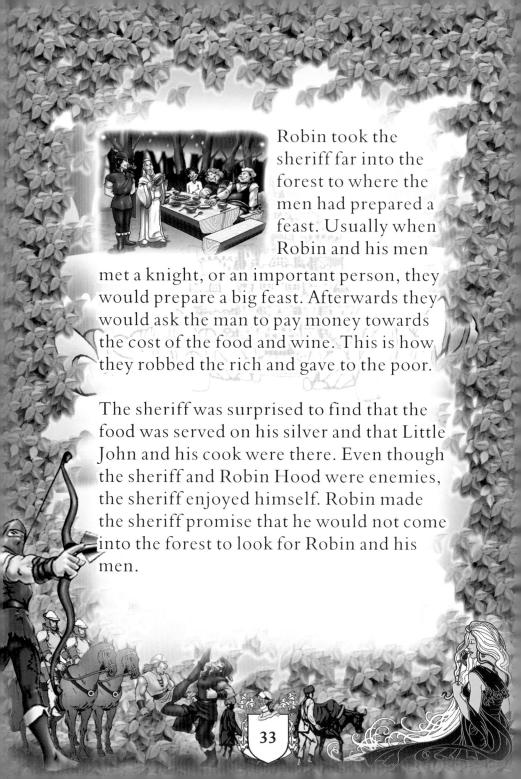

Robin took the sheriff far into the forest to where the men had prepared a feast. Usually when Robin and his men met a knight, or an important person, they would prepare a big feast. Afterwards they would ask the man to pay money towards the cost of the food and wine. This is how they robbed the rich and gave to the poor.

The sheriff was surprised to find that the food was served on his silver and that Little John and his cook were there. Even though the sheriff and Robin Hood were enemies, the sheriff enjoyed himself. Robin made the sheriff promise that he would not come into the forest to look for Robin and his men.

羅賓漢將州長帶到森林裡的深處，他的手下準備了一頓大餐等著。一般說來，羅賓漢和手下遇到爵士或一個重要人物時，都會準備豐盛的一餐待客。之後他們會要求客人付酒飯錢。這是他們劫富濟貧的方法。

州長很驚訝的發現食物是用他的銀器來盛，而且短腳約翰和他的廚師都在那裡。雖然州長和羅賓漢是敵人，州長仍盡情的享用大餐。羅賓漢要州長承諾將不會再到此森林來尋找他和他的人。

The sheriff agreed, but said he could not promise what would happen if Robin and his men left the forest. Lastly, Robin took twenty gold pieces from the sheriff and guided him back to the road so he could find his way home.

州長答應了，但說如果羅賓漢和手下走出此森林，他不保證他們會平安無事。最後羅賓漢從州長那兒取走二十塊金幣，然後將他帶回路上，讓他自行回家。

HOW ROBIN HOOD MET WILL SCARLET

Robin Hood and Little John took a walk in the forest. It was a sunny day and they laid down on the grass. After a few minutes they heard footsteps and someone whistling. Robin decided he was going to take money from the man.

As Robin approached the stranger, the man ignored him and continued to walk. The man was dressed in scarlet clothes and had long blond hair. He looked like a rich man. Robin demanded money, but the man refused. Robin became angry and challenged the man to a fight.

The man gladly agreed. The man was very strong and he managed to beat Robin. As Robin fell to the ground, Little John appeared and stopped the fight.

羅賓漢結識血腥威爾

羅賓漢和短腳約翰在森林中漫步。這一天陽光普照，他們在草地上躺著。幾分鐘後，他們聽見人的腳步聲和吹哨聲。羅賓漢決定要來搶這人的錢。

羅賓漢來到這人面前時，這人並不理會他，只是兀自走著。他身著猩紅色衣服，一頭金色的長髮。他看來像個富人。羅賓漢命令他交出錢來，這人不肯。羅賓漢不甚高興，向這人挑戰比武。

這人愉快的答應。他很強壯，而且使盡全力要打敗羅賓漢。羅賓漢被打倒在地時，短腳約翰出來阻止他們打鬥。

The man listened to Robin and John talking. He recognized Robin. The man introduced himself as Will Gamewell, Robin's old friend, who he had not seen for years. Both men were very happy. Will told Robin that he had come to Sherwood Forest to look for Robin. He wanted to join Robin's men.

He was wanted by the sheriff for killing a man who had stolen from and insulted his father. He was also a outlaw now. Of course Robin agreed. They named him Will Scarlet, because of his clothes, and they set off back into the forest.

這人聽著羅賓漢和約翰談話。他認出了羅賓漢。他自稱威兒'蓋蔚爾。是羅賓漢的舊識，羅賓漢已有多年沒見到他了。這兩人都很開心。威兒告訴羅賓漢他是來雪霧森林找他的。他想加入羅賓漢的行列。

威兒被州長通緝，因爲他殺死了侮辱他父親並偷取父親財物的人。他現在也是一名罪犯。羅賓漢自是答應。因爲他的穿著，他被命名爲血腥威爾。然後他們起身回返森林。

ROBIN GOES TO FIND FRIAR TUCK

Robin Hood always enjoyed a challenge. When he heard about a man who was good at fighting, he would travel to fight him.

One day, Will Scarlet told Robin about Friar Tuck. He was meant to be a great swordsman. Immediately Robin went to find him.

As Robin arrived at a river, he heard voices. Two men were discussing food. When Robin saw them, one was quite fat and Robin wanted to laugh. He took out his bow and arrow and pointed it at the man. Then Robin demanded that the man carry him across the river. The fat man agreed and carried him across.

羅賓漢找尋塔克修道士

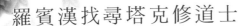

羅賓漢樂於接受挑戰。每當聽說有人善於打鬥時，他便主動去找那個人較量。

這天，血腥威爾向羅賓漢說有關塔克修道士的事。他是天生的劍客高手。羅賓漢立即啓程去找他。

羅賓漢來到一條河前，他聽見人聲。有兩個人在討論食物。羅賓漢瞧見他們時，其中一人身材圓滾滾，他不禁要笑出來。他取出弓箭，瞄準那胖子。羅賓漢命令那人背他過河。胖子同意並背他過河。

When they reached the other side, the man took out his sword and demanded that Robin also carry him across the river. Robin had no choice. It was difficult as Robin did not know the river and the man was very heavy. Eventually he made it across.

On the riverbank, Robin challenged the man to a fight. The man agreed to fight Robin in the middle of the river. They fought and fought until Robin asked if he could blow his horn. Immediately his men appeared. The fat man asked if he could whistle. Immediately many dogs appeared. Everybody began to laugh at the situation.

他們到了河岸邊後，胖子拿出劍，命令羅賓漢也要背他過河。羅賓漢没有別的選擇，只得同意。因爲不熟悉該條河流的緣故，加上胖子的重量，羅賓漢背得很辛苦。但最後他還是做到了。

在河邊羅賓漢向胖子挑戰打鬥。胖子同意在河中間和羅賓漢一較長短。兩人打得難捨難分，最後羅賓漢問他是否可以吹號角。他的手下立即出現了。胖子問他是否可以吹哨子。一下子許多狗出現了。每個人對此景都不禁大笑起來。

Then the man introduced himself as Friar Tuck. Robin was very surprised, this was the man he had been looking for. Robin explained who he was and asked the friar to join him. Friar Tuck accepted happily as he had heard about Robin's good deeds.

胖子自稱是塔克修道士。羅賓漢非常驚訝，原來這就是他要找的人。羅賓漢解釋他的身分，並要求修道士加入他的陣營。修道士愉快的接受了羅賓漢的要求，因爲他早已聽說過羅賓漢的善行。

ROBIN ARRANGES A MARRIAGE

That evening, Friar Tuck and the Sheriff's cook made a wonderful dinner. Afterwards, Robin took a walk in the forest feeling very contented. He heard someone singing. It was a man singing about his lover. As Robin was feeling contented, he decided not to fight the man and continued to walk through the forest.

The next day, Little John and Friar Tuck brought a man to see Robin. It was the man who had been singing the previous night. However, today his clothes were torn and he was very unhappy. His name was Allan-O-Dale.

羅賓漢安排婚禮

當天晚上塔克修道士和州長的廚師做出一頓美味佳餚。之後羅賓漢在森林裡散步，心裡感到非常滿足。他聽到有人在唱歌。這男人唱著心上人的歌。羅賓漢因爲心滿意足，也就不想找這人一較高下，只是繼續在森林中的漫步。

第二天，短腳約翰和塔克修道士帶了一個人來見羅賓漢。他便是前一個晚上在唱歌的那個男人。然而，他今天看起來很不快樂，身上衣服亦是破爛不堪。他的名字是艾倫'歐戴爾。

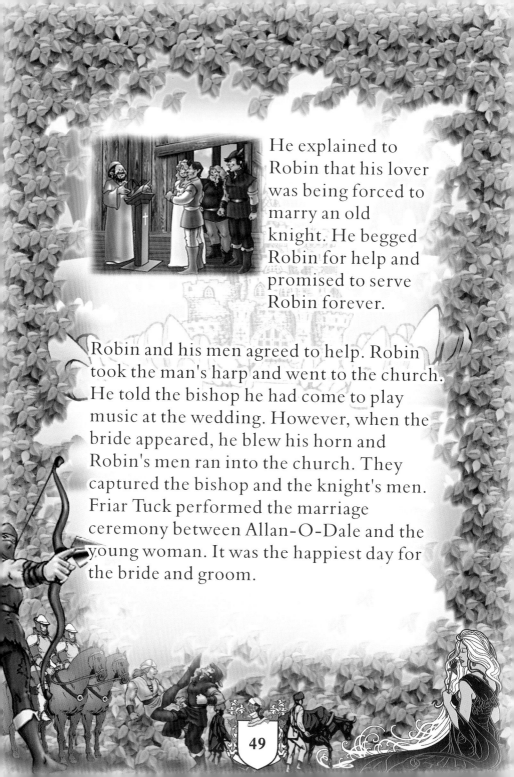

He explained to Robin that his lover was being forced to marry an old knight. He begged Robin for help and promised to serve Robin forever.

Robin and his men agreed to help. Robin took the man's harp and went to the church. He told the bishop he had come to play music at the wedding. However, when the bride appeared, he blew his horn and Robin's men ran into the church. They captured the bishop and the knight's men. Friar Tuck performed the marriage ceremony between Allan-O-Dale and the young woman. It was the happiest day for the bride and groom.

他向羅賓漢道出事情的原委，他的愛人被迫嫁給一名年老的爵士。他向羅賓漢懇求幫助，並承諾將服侍羅賓漢一輩子。

羅賓漢和他的手下同意幫忙。羅賓漢拿了他的豎琴到了教堂。他告訴主教他是來爲婚禮伴奏的。不過新娘一出現的時候，羅賓漢吹號角，他的手下湧進了教堂。他們將主教和爵士的人全抓住。塔克修道士爲年輕的女郎和艾倫主持婚禮。這是新郎和新娘最快樂的一天。

THREE MEN ARE CAPTURED AND RESCUED

After the wedding ceremony, Robin locked the bishop and the wedding party in the church. They did not escape until the morning.

The bishop was so angry he went to the sheriff and demanded that Robin Hood be arrested. The sheriff did not want to go into the forest, but the bishop said he would go to the king if the sheriff did not agree. The sheriff sent all his men to the forest. There they found a group of Robin's men. They had a good fight, but unfortunately three of Robin's men were captured.

羅賓漢的三名手下被抓和被救的過程

婚禮過後，羅賓漢將主教和其他參加婚禮的人全鎖在教堂裡。這些人一直到了隔天早晨才逃脫。

主教非常氣怒，他到州長那裡去，要求州長逮捕羅賓漢。州長不願到那森林裡去，但是主教表示如果州長不去，他將請國王定奪。於是州長派出所有的人到森林裡去。他們在那裡找到羅賓漢的一群手下。雙方展開一場大戰，不幸的是羅賓漢的三名手下被擄獲。

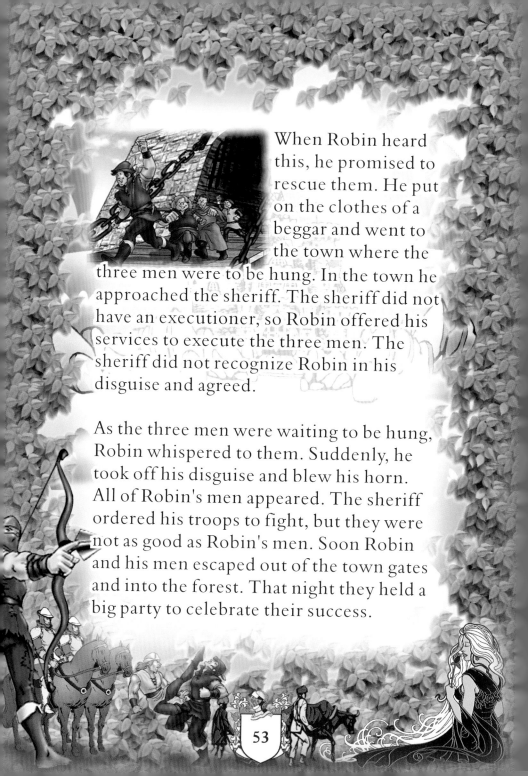

When Robin heard this, he promised to rescue them. He put on the clothes of a beggar and went to the town where the three men were to be hung. In the town he approached the sheriff. The sheriff did not have an executioner, so Robin offered his services to execute the three men. The sheriff did not recognize Robin in his disguise and agreed.

As the three men were waiting to be hung, Robin whispered to them. Suddenly, he took off his disguise and blew his horn. All of Robin's men appeared. The sheriff ordered his troops to fight, but they were not as good as Robin's men. Soon Robin and his men escaped out of the town gates and into the forest. That night they held a big party to celebrate their success.

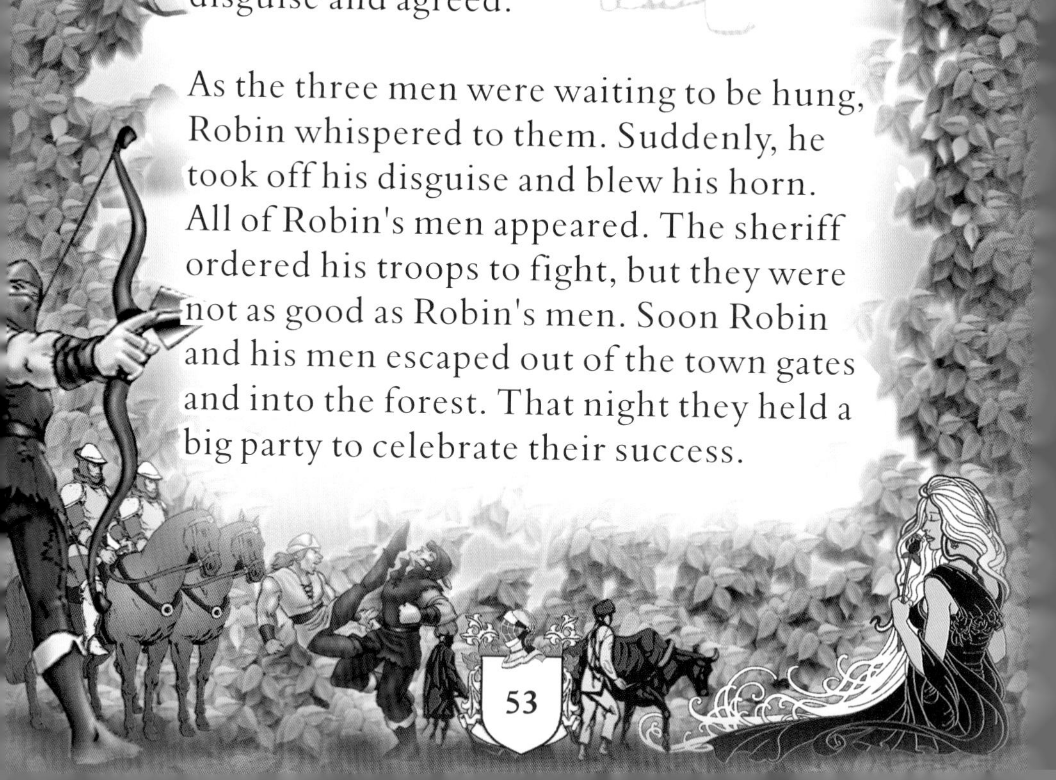

羅賓漢聽說此事，決心將他們救回來。他扮成一名乞丐進城，向三名手下即將被處以絞刑的地方前進。到了城裡，羅賓漢走向州長那兒。因爲州長沒有行刑的人，羅賓漢便主動要求處死那三人。州長沒認出喬裝後的羅賓漢，於是答應了。

那三人在等著被處死時。羅賓漢對他們低聲說了些話。突然他摘下他的假扮，大鳴號角。羅賓漢所有的手下全來到了。州長命手下與他們交戰，但是州長的手下打不過羅賓漢的人。沒多久羅賓漢就帶著手下逃出城門，躲進森林裡了。該晚他們舉行了一個盛大的宴會慶祝他們的勝利。

ROBIN IS OUTWITTED BY A BEGGAR

Robin was walking through the forest, as usual, one morning when he saw a beggar. Even though the man was badly dressed, he was quite fat and was carrying a large purse. Robin decided to take some of his money. He approached the beggar, but the beggar continued walking.

Robin demanded money, but the beggar refused. Robin took his stick out and prepared to fight. However, the beggar was very quick and beat the stick from Robin's hands. Robin had no choice but to run away.

Robin blew his horn and three of his men appeared. Robin told them what had happened and the men ran after the beggar.

乞丐智勝羅賓漢

這天早晨羅賓漢一如往常在森林裡行走，這次他遇見一名乞丐。雖然這名乞丐穿得寒酸，身材卻很肥胖，而且帶著一個大錢包。羅賓漢想來搶這個人的一些錢。他走近乞丐身邊，乞丐則是自顧自的走著。

羅賓漢命令他交出錢來，乞丐不依。羅賓漢取出竹棍，準備和他較量一番。然而，乞丐卻身手很快，將羅賓漢手中的竹棍打落。羅賓漢只得逃走。

羅賓漢吹號角召出三名手下。羅賓漢告訴他們這件事，他的手下於是前去追趕乞丐。

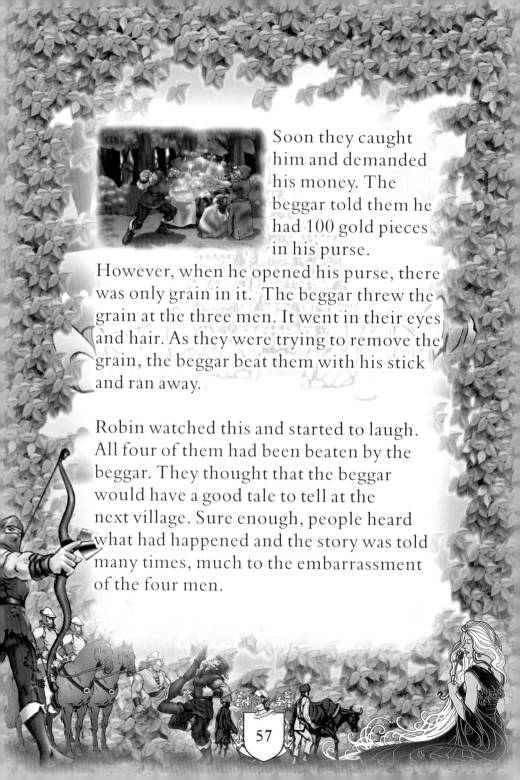

Soon they caught him and demanded his money. The beggar told them he had 100 gold pieces in his purse. However, when he opened his purse, there was only grain in it. The beggar threw the grain at the three men. It went in their eyes and hair. As they were trying to remove the grain, the beggar beat them with his stick and ran away.

Robin watched this and started to laugh. All four of them had been beaten by the beggar. They thought that the beggar would have a good tale to tell at the next village. Sure enough, people heard what had happened and the story was told many times, much to the embarrassment of the four men.

不久他們追上了乞丐，並要他交出身上的財物。乞丐說他的錢包裡有一百塊金幣。但是他打開錢包時，裡面有的只是穀子。乞丐將穀子灑向那三名手下。穀子跑進他們的眼睛和頭髮裡。他們試著撥去穀粒，乞丐則趁機用手杖打他們，然後逃之夭夭。

羅賓漢看到這裡不禁哈哈大笑。他們四人全被那乞丐給打敗了。他們認爲那乞丐將會有一個很好的故事可以告訴他到的下一個村莊。果不其然，人們聽說了這個故事，並傳頌了許多次，讓羅賓漢四人非常尷尬。

ROBIN MEETS GUY OF GISBANE AND RESCUES LITTLE JOHN

By now the king had heard about Robin Hood. He told the sheriff that if Robin was not captured, the sheriff would lose his job. The king offered a reward to the man who captured Robin.

One of the king's men had also heard about Robin and the reward that was offered for capturing him. This man was called Guy of Gisbane. Guy went to Nottingham and told the sheriff that he would find Robin. He said he would go alone. When he found Robin, he would blow his horn and the sheriff must come immediately.

吉斯本的凱依與羅賓漢纏鬥，羅賓漢救出短腳約翰

如今國王已聽說了羅賓漢的事。他對州長表示如果抓不到羅賓漢，他這個州長也別做了。對能抓到羅賓漢的人，國王將給予賞賜。

國王的一個手下也聽說了羅賓漢的事和國王的懸賞。這個人是來自吉斯本的凱依。凱依到那汀罕告訴州長他將找到羅賓漢。他表示要獨自行動。找到羅賓漢的時候，他會吹號角，州長必須立即趕來。

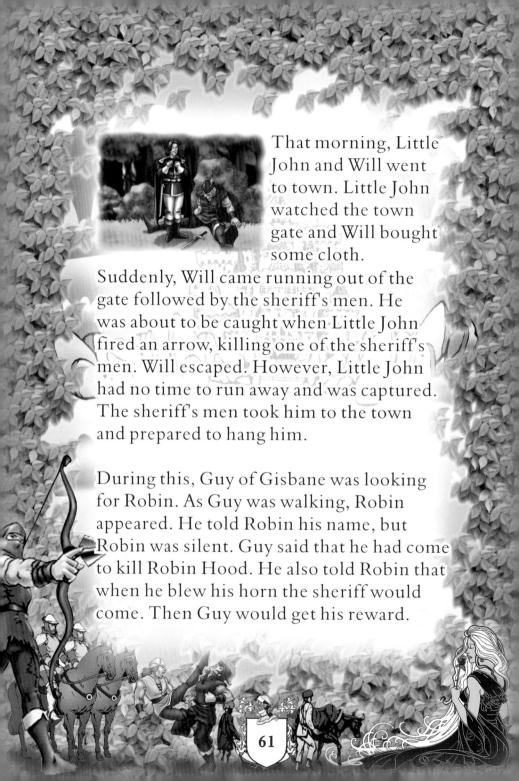

That morning, Little John and Will went to town. Little John watched the town gate and Will bought some cloth.

Suddenly, Will came running out of the gate followed by the sheriff's men. He was about to be caught when Little John fired an arrow, killing one of the sheriff's men. Will escaped. However, Little John had no time to run away and was captured. The sheriff's men took him to the town and prepared to hang him.

During this, Guy of Gisbane was looking for Robin. As Guy was walking, Robin appeared. He told Robin his name, but Robin was silent. Guy said that he had come to kill Robin Hood. He also told Robin that when he blew his horn the sheriff would come. Then Guy would get his reward.

那天早晨，短腳約翰和威爾到城裡去。短腳約翰監視著城門，威爾去買些布料。突然間，威爾從城門內奔出，後頭追著州長的人。就在他快要被抓到的時候，短腳約翰用箭射死了州長的一名手下。威爾逃脫了。但是短腳約翰因爲來不及逃開而被捉住了。州長的人將他抓進城裡，準備將他處以絞刑。

同時間，吉斯本的凱依四處尋找羅賓漢。當凱依在行走的時候，羅賓漢出現了。他告訴羅賓漢自己的名字，羅賓漢沈默以對。凱依說他是來殺羅賓漢的。他又說只要他一吹號角，州長就會出現。然後凱依就能拿到獎賞了。

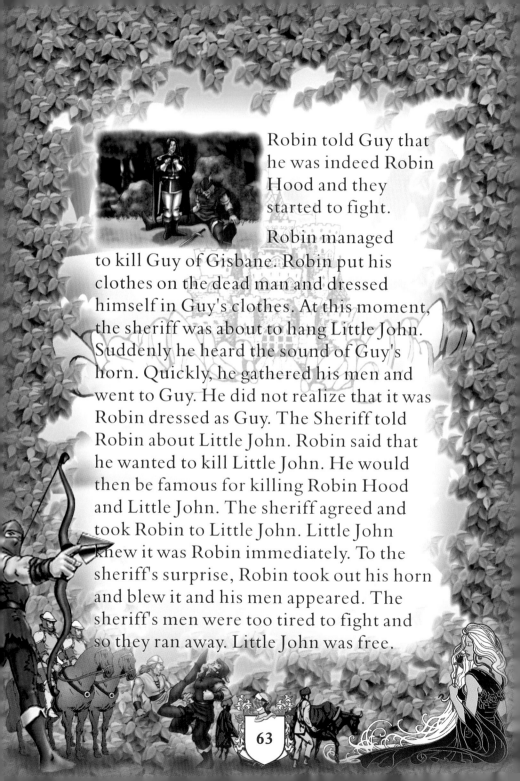

Robin told Guy that he was indeed Robin Hood and they started to fight.

Robin managed to kill Guy of Gisbane. Robin put his clothes on the dead man and dressed himself in Guy's clothes. At this moment, the sheriff was about to hang Little John. Suddenly he heard the sound of Guy's horn. Quickly, he gathered his men and went to Guy. He did not realize that it was Robin dressed as Guy. The Sheriff told Robin about Little John. Robin said that he wanted to kill Little John. He would then be famous for killing Robin Hood and Little John. The sheriff agreed and took Robin to Little John. Little John knew it was Robin immediately. To the sheriff's surprise, Robin took out his horn and blew it and his men appeared. The sheriff's men were too tired to fight and so they ran away. Little John was free.

羅賓漢向凱依說他正是羅賓漢，兩人於是打了起來。

最後羅賓漢好不容易殺死凱依。羅賓漢將自己的衣服穿在已死的凱依身上，然後換上凱依的服裝。此時此刻州長即將吊死短腳約翰。突然間，他聽見凱依的號角聲。於是他迅速地召集好人馬，往凱依的方向去了。州長未察覺凱依是羅賓漢假扮的。州長告訴羅賓漢短腳約翰的事。羅賓漢說他要親手殺了短腳約翰。然後他將以殺死羅賓漢和短腳約翰聞名。州長同意並帶羅賓漢到短腳約翰那裡。短腳約翰立即認出羅賓漢。讓州長大感驚訝的是，羅賓漢拿出他的號角嗚吹，召來他的人馬。州長的手下此時已是兵倦馬疲，紛紛逃走。短腳約翰重獲自由。

MARION AND ROBIN MEET AGAIN

One morning Robin was hunting deer. He was in disguise and he was thinking about Marion. He missed her and wished with all his heart to see her again. Suddenly he saw a deer, but before he could fire an arrow, the deer fell down dead.

From the other side of the forest a man appeared. Robin approached him and told the man that he should not shoot the king's animals. The man was quite rude to Robin and took out his sword. Robin had no choice and fought the man. After fighting for a while, Robin allowed the man to cut him so the fight would end.

瑪莉安和羅賓漢重逢

有天早晨羅賓漢出外狩獵鹿隻。喬裝改扮的他正在思念著瑪莉安。他想念她，滿心希望再見到她。突然他看見一隻鹿，但是他還來不及射出箭的時候，該隻鹿已倒地死去。

一個人從森林的另一端出現。羅賓漢走向他說，他不應該射殺國王的動物。那人對羅賓漢相當無禮，並取出他的劍。羅賓漢不得不和那人較量一番。格鬥了一陣子，羅賓漢讓對方殺了他一刀，一場打鬥才停止。

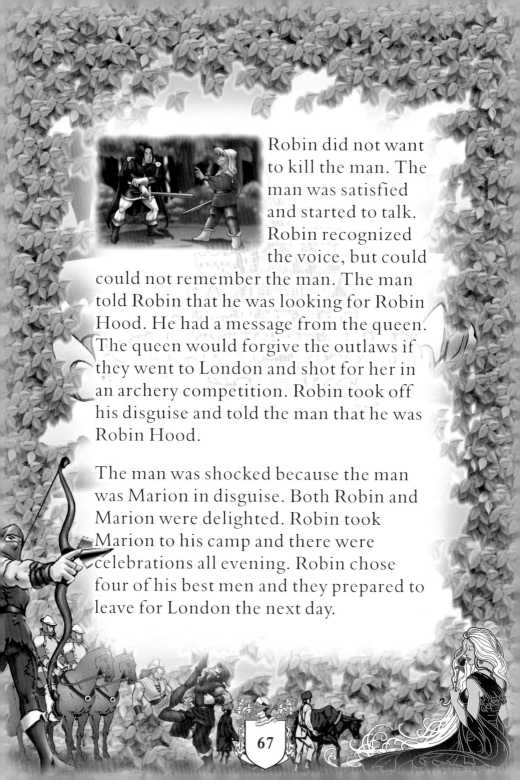

Robin did not want to kill the man. The man was satisfied and started to talk. Robin recognized the voice, but could could not remember the man. The man told Robin that he was looking for Robin Hood. He had a message from the queen. The queen would forgive the outlaws if they went to London and shot for her in an archery competition. Robin took off his disguise and told the man that he was Robin Hood.

The man was shocked because the man was Marion in disguise. Both Robin and Marion were delighted. Robin took Marion to his camp and there were celebrations all evening. Robin chose four of his best men and they prepared to leave for London the next day.

羅賓漢並不打算殺了對方。而那人由於心滿意足，於是開始和羅賓漢聊了起來。羅賓漢覺得他的聲音很熟悉，卻記不得是誰。對方表示他正在尋找羅賓漢。他帶著皇后的口信。如果這些罪犯肯到倫敦，參加射箭比賽，皇后將會原諒他們。羅賓漢揭開他的裝扮，並告訴對方他就是羅賓漢。

那人很震驚，因爲他是女扮男裝的瑪莉安。羅賓漢及瑪莉安兩人都極爲興奮。羅賓漢帶著瑪莉安回到他的營地，整晚慶祝的活動不斷。羅賓漢選了四名精英，他們四人將在第二天遠赴倫敦。

THE ARCHERY COMPETITION

The competition was a grand affair. Everyone was dressed in their finest clothes and were talking and laughing. The king and queen arrived, followed by the King's archers. The king's servant announced that the first round would decide who was the best of the king's archers. The second round would decide who was the best archer in the country.

Before the second round, the queen told the king that she had five archers who would shoot for her. She wanted her archers to compete against the best five archers of the king. The king agreed and he bet five hundred pounds that his archers would win. The queen also asked that if her men won, they would be given their freedom.

射箭比賽

這場射箭比賽是件大事。每個人都穿出最華麗的服飾，談笑風生。國王和皇后抵達時，一群國王的弓箭手在後頭跟隨著。國王的僕人宣佈第一回合的比賽將決定誰是國王最好的弓箭手。第二回合的比賽將決定誰是全國第一。

第二回合開始前，皇后對國王說，她有五名弓箭手將爲她射箭。她要她的人和國王的前五名弓箭手比賽。國王同意，並下注五百塊金幣，賭他的弓箭手贏。皇后也要求若她的人贏了，他們必須得到自由。

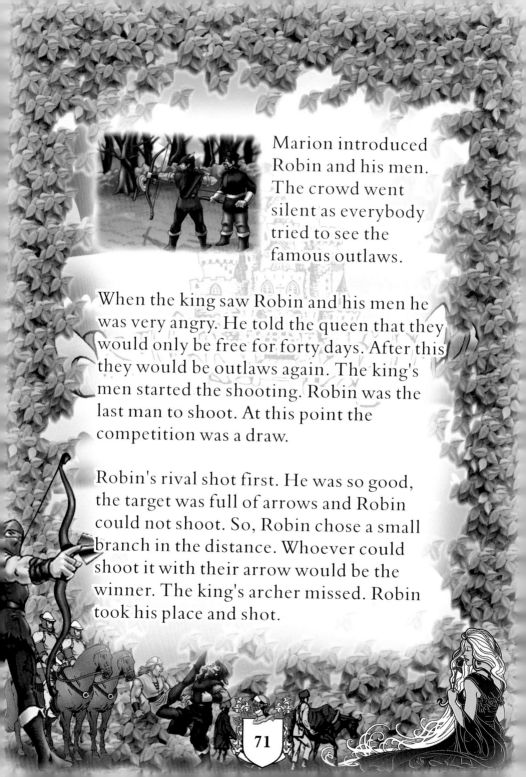

Marion introduced Robin and his men. The crowd went silent as everybody tried to see the famous outlaws.

When the king saw Robin and his men he was very angry. He told the queen that they would only be free for forty days. After this they would be outlaws again. The king's men started the shooting. Robin was the last man to shoot. At this point the competition was a draw.

Robin's rival shot first. He was so good, the target was full of arrows and Robin could not shoot. So, Robin chose a small branch in the distance. Whoever could shoot it with their arrow would be the winner. The king's archer missed. Robin took his place and shot.

國王看到羅賓漢和他的人時，非常的憤怒。他告訴皇后，這些人將只有四十天的自由。在那之後，他們將恢復罪犯的身份。國王的手下先開始。羅賓漢是最後射的人。比賽到此，雙方不分勝負。

羅賓漢的對手先射箭。他的技術很好，靶上滿是箭支，使得羅賓漢無法射靶。因此羅賓漢選擇遠方的一截小樹枝。凡是能射中那樹枝的人便是贏家。國王的弓箭手沒射中。羅賓漢上場，箭出弓後。

The arrow went straight through the branch and split it in two. When the king saw this, he left immediately.

The outlaws were given their prizes, money and a silver bugle. They were also given food and wine. However, they gave the food and wine to the king's archers. This made them very popular and they talked and laughed with the king's men.

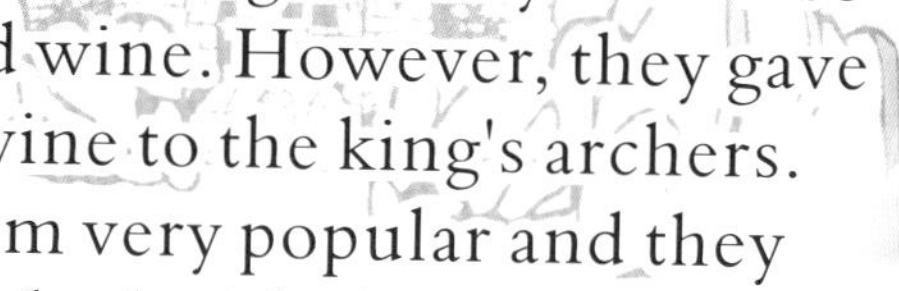

箭支直直穿過，樹枝斷成兩截。看到這裡，國王立即離去。

羅賓漢一行人獲頒獎品、獎金、一個銀製的號角。他們還被給予食物和酒。但是他們將食物和酒轉送給國王的弓箭手。這一舉動使他們備受歡迎。他們並和國王的手下一同談天說笑。

ROBIN AND THE TINKER

Forty days after the archery competition, the king kept his promise and renewed his search for Robin.

The sheriff did not know what to do. He had been to the forest three times, but could not find Robin. The sheriff's daughter also hated Robin and she was determined to capture him. One day, the sheriff's daughter heard the tinker talking about Robin Hood. As he was mending the pots and pans he was saying that he could find Robin. Immediately she told him that she would give him money to capture Robin.

羅賓漢和補鍋匠

射箭比賽後的四十天過去了，國王依照他曾說過的話，開始重新搜尋羅賓漢。

州長卻不知道該怎麼做。他已經去過森林裡三次，都未能找到羅賓漢。州長的女兒也討厭羅賓漢。她決定要擒拿住他。一天州長的女兒聽到一個補鍋匠在談論著羅賓漢。他一邊修補鍋子，一邊說他有辦法找到羅賓漢。州長的女兒立即告訴他，只要抓到羅賓漢，他就有錢可拿。

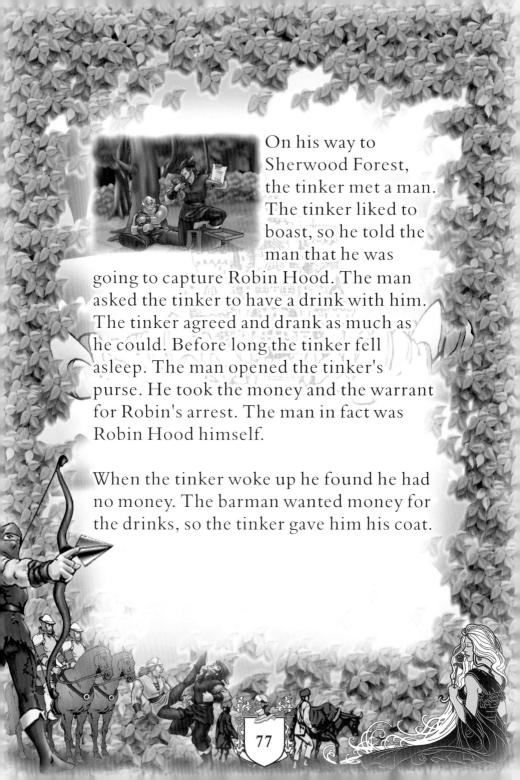

On his way to Sherwood Forest, the tinker met a man. The tinker liked to boast, so he told the man that he was going to capture Robin Hood. The man asked the tinker to have a drink with him. The tinker agreed and drank as much as he could. Before long the tinker fell asleep. The man opened the tinker's purse. He took the money and the warrant for Robin's arrest. The man in fact was Robin Hood himself.

When the tinker woke up he found he had no money. The barman wanted money for the drinks, so the tinker gave him his coat.

在前往雪霧森林的途中，補鍋匠遇見一個人。這名補鍋匠一向喜歡誇口，於是就說他將去捉拿羅賓漢。對方要補鍋匠和他一起喝酒。補鍋匠答應了，而且喝個不停。過不了多久他就醉倒了。那人將補鍋匠的提箱打開。他取走了錢和逮捕羅賓漢的逮捕令。事實上這個人就是羅賓漢。

補鍋匠酒醒之後發現身上毫無分文。酒吧的人跟他要酒錢，補鍋匠只得給了他的外套。

The tinker left the inn in a very bad mood. As he walked down the road he saw Robin. The tinker ran to Robin and began to hit him. Robin blew his horn and soon Little John and Will arrived. Robin gave the tinker his money and the tinker was pleased. He asked if he could join Robin and his men. He forgot all about the sheriff's daughter and capturing Robin.

補鍋匠離開客棧時心情壞透了。在路上遇見了羅賓漢。補鍋匠跑向羅賓漢，開始打他。羅賓漢吹號角，很快地短腳約翰和威爾都來到。羅賓漢把錢還給補鍋匠，補鍋匠很高興。他問自己是否可以加入羅賓漢的行列。他已經將州長女兒的話和逮捕羅賓漢的事忘得一乾二淨了。

THE TANNER MEETS ROBIN AND LITTLE JOHN

The sheriff's daughter waited for the tinker to return. When she realized that he was not coming back, she sent for Arthur-a-Bland. He was a tanner, making clothes from animal skins. He was famous throughout the county for fighting with a stick. The sheriff's daughter asked Arthur to find Robin Hood. Arthur was happy to do this because it meant he could also kill some deer in the forest.

On the same day that Arthur set off for Sherwood Forest, Robin and Little John went to the market. Little John was going to buy some cloth for winter clothes. Robin stayed in the forest while Little John was buying the cloth. While he was waiting, Robin saw Arthur shoot a deer.

製革匠遇見羅賓漢和短腳約翰

州長的女兒一直等著補鍋匠回來。當她了解到補鍋匠不會再回來時，她改派亞瑟·別倫。他是個製革匠，專用動物皮革製衣的人。他善於用棍棒打鬥，因而聞名全國。州長的女兒命亞瑟去尋找羅賓漢。亞瑟樂於接受這差事，因爲這表示他也可以在森林裡捕殺些鹿隻。

亞瑟出發到雪霧森林的同一天，羅賓漢和短腳約翰則要到市集去。短腳約翰要買些冬衣的布料。短腳約翰去買布料的時候，羅賓漢在森林裡等著。羅賓漢在等的時候，看見製革匠正在獵殺一隻鹿。

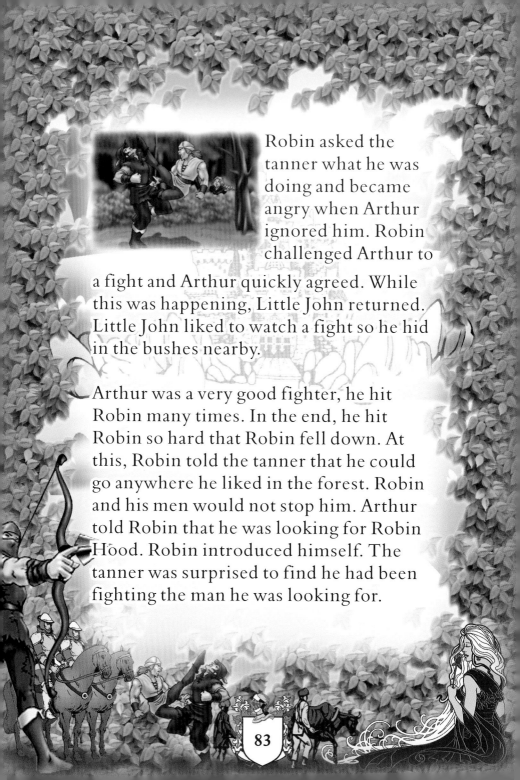

Robin asked the tanner what he was doing and became angry when Arthur ignored him. Robin challenged Arthur to a fight and Arthur quickly agreed. While this was happening, Little John returned. Little John liked to watch a fight so he hid in the bushes nearby.

Arthur was a very good fighter, he hit Robin many times. In the end, he hit Robin so hard that Robin fell down. At this, Robin told the tanner that he could go anywhere he liked in the forest. Robin and his men would not stop him. Arthur told Robin that he was looking for Robin Hood. Robin introduced himself. The tanner was surprised to find he had been fighting the man he was looking for.

羅賓漢問製革匠他在做什麼，亞瑟不予理會，使得羅賓漢很不高興。羅賓漢向亞瑟挑戰，亞瑟很快的答應了。這一切發生時，短腳約翰已經返回。因爲短腳約翰喜歡觀看打鬥，於是他藏在附近的灌木叢裡。

亞瑟是個很厲害的打者，他擊中羅賓漢許多次。最後他對羅賓漢施以重擊，使得羅賓漢跌在地上。至此羅賓漢告訴製革匠，說他可以自由在森林中遊走。羅賓漢和他的人將不會阻擋他。亞瑟說他是來找羅賓漢的。羅賓漢對他自我介紹。亞瑟很驚訝和他格鬥的人竟然就是他要找的人。

Arthur asked Robin where Little John was. He was a relation of Little John. On hearing this, Little John came out of the bushes. The tanner was very pleased to see him. Arthur asked if he could join Robin's men. Robin welcomed him because they could use his skills.

亞瑟問羅賓漢短腳約翰人在何處。他是短腳約翰的親戚。聽到這裡，短腳約翰從灌木叢中走出。製革匠見到他很開心。亞瑟並問他是否可以加入羅賓漢的人。羅賓漢很歡迎他，因爲他們可以借用他的手藝。

SIR RICHARD AND MARION ARRIVE

As Robin was walking through the forest he was attacked by a deer. As he was getting ready to shoot the animal, Marion appeared. She did not see the deer and it ran towards her. The deer knocked Marion to the ground and prepared to attack again. Robin shouted to Marion to lie still. With great accuracy, Robin shot the deer between the eyes.

When Marion recovered, she and Robin rejoiced at being together again. Marion told Robin what had happened to her. King Henry was dead and Richard the Lion Heart was now king. However, King Richard was away fighting and his brother, John, had taken his place.

理察爵士和瑪莉安的駕臨

羅賓漢在森林中行走的時候遭受到一隻鹿的攻擊。他正準備射鹿的時候，瑪莉安出現了。她並未看見該隻鹿，鹿卻朝她的方向奔去。該隻鹿將瑪莉安衝撞在地後，又準備再次攻擊。羅賓漢高聲叫瑪莉安躺在地上別動。羅賓漢極準確的將箭射進鹿的兩眼之間。

瑪莉安回過神來，她與羅賓漢對於再次相逢都欣喜若狂。瑪莉安對羅賓漢訴說發生在她身邊的一些事。亨利國王駕崩，獅心理察繼任爲王。但是理察國王出征時，他的兄弟約翰趁機篡位。

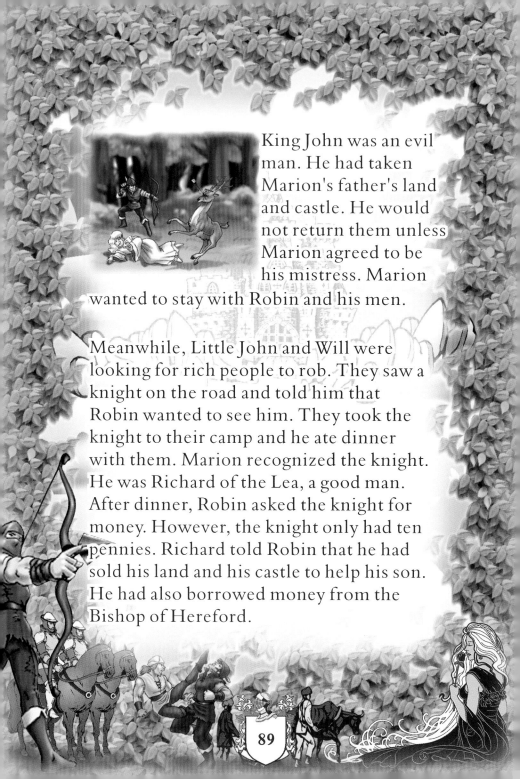

King John was an evil man. He had taken Marion's father's land and castle. He would not return them unless Marion agreed to be his mistress. Marion wanted to stay with Robin and his men.

Meanwhile, Little John and Will were looking for rich people to rob. They saw a knight on the road and told him that Robin wanted to see him. They took the knight to their camp and he ate dinner with them. Marion recognized the knight. He was Richard of the Lea, a good man. After dinner, Robin asked the knight for money. However, the knight only had ten pennies. Richard told Robin that he had sold his land and his castle to help his son. He had also borrowed money from the Bishop of Hereford.

約翰國王是個邪惡的人。他從瑪莉安的父親那裡掠奪了土地和城堡。除非瑪莉安同意做他的情婦，否則他是不會歸還那些財產的。瑪莉安希望留在羅賓漢和其手下的身邊。

在此同時，短腳約翰和威爾在尋找富人好搶錢。他們在路上見到一爵士，便告訴他羅賓漢想見他。他們將爵士帶到營地，請他吃飯。瑪莉安認出這個爵士。他是李縣的理察，是個好人。用完餐，羅賓漢跟這個爵士要錢。但是爵士身上只有十便士。理察告訴羅賓漢他為了幫助兒子，才售出他的土地和城堡。他尚且向曦拂主教借了錢。

Little John approached with a large sack. From the sack he gave the knight four hundred pounds. This was the amount Richard owed the Bishop of Hereford. He also gave the knight some clothes and a new horse. The knight almost cried through joy. He promised that before the end of the year he would repay the money.

短腳約翰取來一只大袋子。他從袋子裡拿出四百塊金幣給了爵士。這是理察向曦拂主教借錢的數目。他並給了爵士一些衣服和一匹新馬。爵士幾乎喜極而泣。他承諾將在年底前歸還這筆錢。

THE BISHOP OF HEREFORD PAYS A VISIT

Arthur brought the news to Robin that the Bishop of Hereford would travel past Sherwood Forest that day. Robin sent his men to guard all of the roads. Robin and some of the men disguised themselves as shepherds and killed a deer. They started to cook the deer by the side of the road.

Before long, the bishop and his men arrived. When he saw Robin cooking the deer he stopped. He was angry with Robin for killing the king's deer. Quickly Robin blew his horn and the rest of his men arrived. The bishop could do nothing.

曦拂主教的造訪

這一天，亞瑟聽說曦拂主教將穿過雪霧森林，便將消息通報了羅賓漢。羅賓漢派人看守每一條路。羅賓漢和一些手下則裝扮成牧羊人的模樣，並殺了一隻鹿。他們在路旁烹煮起鹿來。

不久主教和他的人來到。當他看見羅賓漢烹煮著鹿，便停下來了。他對羅賓漢殺了國王的鹿感到憤怒。羅賓漢隨即吹起號角，他的其他手下全部來到。主教無計可施。

Robin led him to their camp and they ate dinner. Afterwards, Robin asked the bishop for money. The bishop was greedy and told Robin that he only had a little money. However, when Little John opened the bishop's bag, there was four hundred gold pieces in it. This was the money that Robin had given Richard of Lea to pay the bishop. Robin took the money. By now the bishop was drunk, so Little John tied him to his horse and sent the horse towards Nottingham.

羅賓漢帶著主教到他們的營地去一同進餐。餐後羅賓漢向主教索取費用。主教是個貪婪的人，於是告訴羅賓漢他只帶著一點錢。但是短腳約翰打開主教的袋子時，裡面裝有四百塊金幣。這些錢是羅賓漢給理察用來償還主教的錢。羅賓漢取走那筆錢。這時主教已是爛醉，所以短腳約翰將他綁在馬上，將他送回那汀罕。

THE BISHOP OF HEREFORD LOOKS FOR ROBIN

Robin thought that the Bishop of Hereford was a coward. He did not believe that the bishop would come back to the woods to look for him. So, the next day, Robin went for a walk along the highway. When he turned the corner he saw the Bishop of Hereford and his men.

Very quickly, Robin jumped behind the bush and ran through the forest. He came across the house of the old woman. Her sons worked for Robin. The old woman and Robin changed clothes. When the bishop's men arrived, all they saw was an old woman.

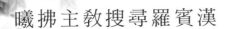

曦拂主教搜尋羅賓漢

羅賓漢認爲曦拂主教是個懦夫。他不相信主教會再回來森林裡找他。所以第二天，羅賓漢在馬路上閒逛。就在走過轉角的那一刹那，他看見曦拂主教和他的手下。

羅賓漢迅速的縱身一躍，跳到灌木叢後，並往森林裡逃去。他途經一老婦人的房子。老婦人的兒子爲羅賓漢工作。老婦人和羅賓漢互相換上對方的衣裳。主教的人來到時，只見老婦人在裡頭。

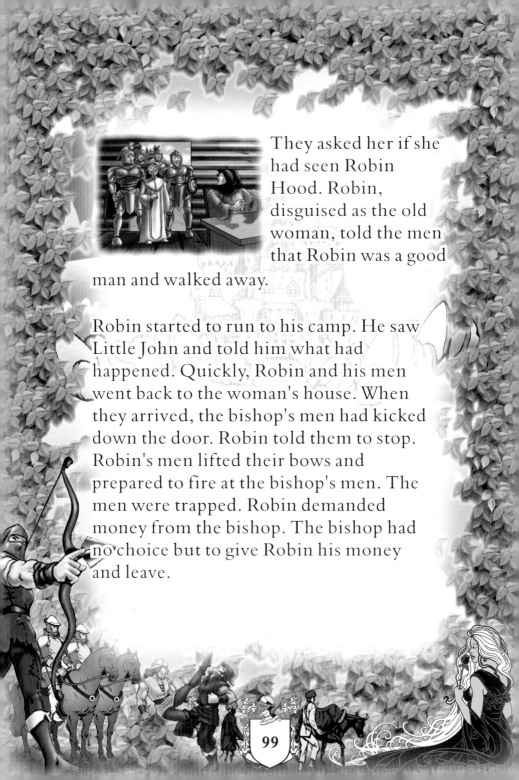

They asked her if she had seen Robin Hood. Robin, disguised as the old woman, told the men that Robin was a good man and walked away.

Robin started to run to his camp. He saw Little John and told him what had happened. Quickly, Robin and his men went back to the woman's house. When they arrived, the bishop's men had kicked down the door. Robin told them to stop. Robin's men lifted their bows and prepared to fire at the bishop's men. The men were trapped. Robin demanded money from the bishop. The bishop had no choice but to give Robin his money and leave.

他們問她是否見到羅賓漢。僞裝成老婦人的羅賓漢告訴那些人，羅賓漢是個好人，便走開了。

羅賓漢逃回他的駐紮地。他見到短腳約翰時，對他說出事情的經過。很快的，羅賓漢和他的人回到老婦人的屋子。他們抵達時，主教的手下已將大門踢倒。羅賓漢要他們住手。羅賓漢的手下舉起弓箭，準備對主教的人射箭。主教的人已被困。羅賓漢向主教索費。主教只得給羅賓漢錢，然後離開。

THE SHERIFF HOLDS ANOTHER ARCHERY COMPETITION

The sheriff was desperate to catch Robin. He went to see King John and ask for help. However, King John only laughed at him. The sheriff returned to Nottingham in low spirits.

The sheriff's daughter had an idea. She told the sheriff to hold an archery competition. She also told him to lie and say that everybody was welcome and that nobody would be captured. The sheriff thought that this was a good idea. He knew that Robin would come to the competition. The sheriff planned to capture Robin at the competition.

州長舉辦另一場射箭比賽

州長對逮捕羅賓漢一事傷透了腦筋。他前去見約翰國王，請求幫助。但是約翰國王只是嘲笑他。州長頹喪的返回那汀罕。

州長的女兒有一個辦法。她叫州長舉行一個射箭比賽。她並叫他撒謊，說歡迎每個人來參加比賽，沒有人會被抓。州長認為這是個好主意。他知道羅賓漢會來參加比賽。州長計畫在比賽時逮捕羅賓漢。

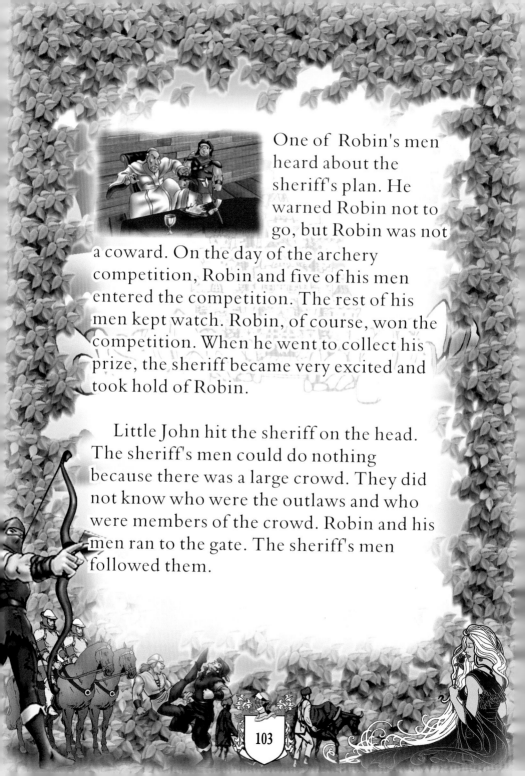

One of Robin's men heard about the sheriff's plan. He warned Robin not to go, but Robin was not a coward. On the day of the archery competition, Robin and five of his men entered the competition. The rest of his men kept watch. Robin, of course, won the competition. When he went to collect his prize, the sheriff became very excited and took hold of Robin.

Little John hit the sheriff on the head. The sheriff's men could do nothing because there was a large crowd. They did not know who were the outlaws and who were members of the crowd. Robin and his men ran to the gate. The sheriff's men followed them.

羅賓漢的一名手下聽說了州長的計畫。他警告羅賓漢別去，但是羅賓漢並非一個懦夫。射箭比賽舉行當天，羅賓漢和五名手下參加了比賽。其他的手下則警戒在側。不出所料，羅賓漢贏得了勝利。在他上前領獎的時候，州長變得很激動，並將羅賓漢抓住。

短腳約翰朝著州長的頭打了過去。州長的人卻無計可施，因爲在場的群衆很多。他們無法分辨哪些人是罪犯，哪些人是圍觀者。羅賓漢等人逃到城門邊。州長的人則尾隨在後。

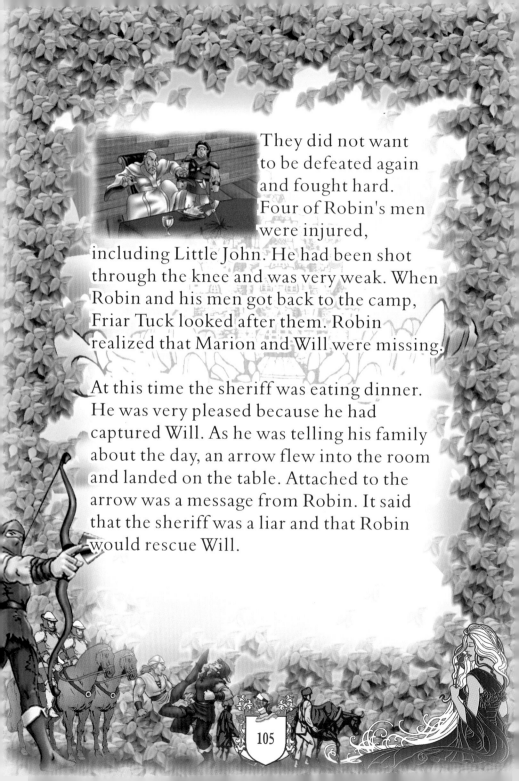

They did not want to be defeated again and fought hard. Four of Robin's men were injured, including Little John. He had been shot through the knee and was very weak. When Robin and his men got back to the camp, Friar Tuck looked after them. Robin realized that Marion and Will were missing.

At this time the sheriff was eating dinner. He was very pleased because he had captured Will. As he was telling his family about the day, an arrow flew into the room and landed on the table. Attached to the arrow was a message from Robin. It said that the sheriff was a liar and that Robin would rescue Will.

他們爲了不想再被打敗而戰得分外激烈。羅賓漢的四名手下受傷，包括短腳約翰在內。他的膝蓋被射穿，腿已無力。羅賓漢等人回到營地時，塔克修道士負責照顧他們。羅賓漢這時才發覺瑪莉安和威爾兩人失蹤。

這時候州長正在用餐。他感到很滿意，因爲他已抓到威爾。他正在向家人描述當天發生的事時，一隻箭飛進了房間，落在餐桌上。箭上附著羅賓漢的一封信。信上說州長食言，而羅賓漢將援救威爾。

THE RESCUE OF WILL STUTELY

On the day that Will Stutely was to be hung, the sheriff locked the gates to his castle. No one was allowed in until after the hanging. Robin and his friends waited at the edge of a forest.

Before long they saw a young priest walking along the road. One of Robin's men approached the priest and asked him what was happening. The priest was wearing a hood, which hid his face, and a long coat. The priest informed him that Robin could get into the castle if they went around the back. Arthur-a-Bland climbed the wall at the back of the castle and opened the gate to let Robin and his men inside.

拯救威爾'史塔利的行動

威爾'史塔利將被處以絞刑的這天，州長將城堡的大門鎖起來。在執行絞刑之前，任何人都不准進出。羅賓漢一行人等在森林邊緣。

過了不久，他們看見一個年輕的牧師在路上行走。羅賓漢的一名手下走到牧師身邊，問他發生了什麼事。該名牧師頂著遮住了臉的連衣帽，穿著一件長袍。他說羅賓漢可以進入城堡內，只是得走後門。亞瑟'別倫從城堡後面翻牆而入，然後打開城門讓羅賓漢和手下進入。

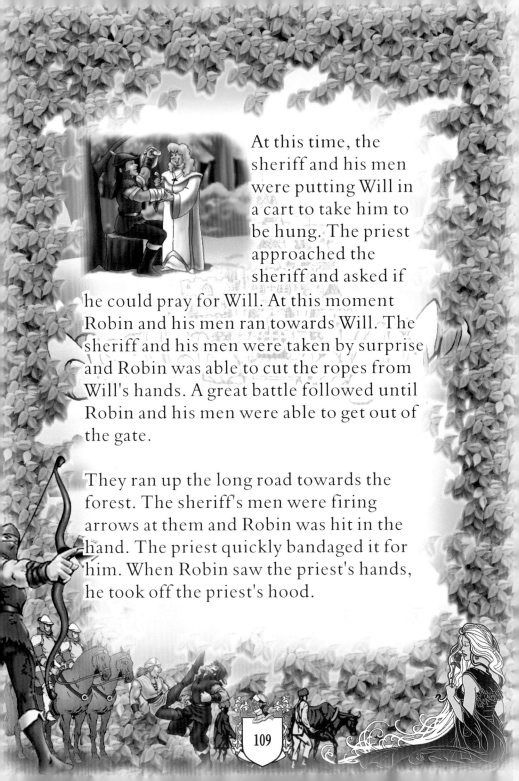

At this time, the sheriff and his men were putting Will in a cart to take him to be hung. The priest approached the sheriff and asked if he could pray for Will. At this moment Robin and his men ran towards Will. The sheriff and his men were taken by surprise and Robin was able to cut the ropes from Will's hands. A great battle followed until Robin and his men were able to get out of the gate.

They ran up the long road towards the forest. The sheriff's men were firing arrows at them and Robin was hit in the hand. The priest quickly bandaged it for him. When Robin saw the priest's hands, he took off the priest's hood.

此刻州長和他的人正要把威爾放到推車裡，以便帶到刑場。那位牧師走向州長，問他是否可以爲威爾禱告。剎時間羅賓漢和手下奔向威爾。州長和他的人都大吃一驚，羅賓漢則藉機切斷綁住威爾雙手的繩索。接下來雙方發生激戰，最後羅賓漢和其手下仍得以逃出城門。

他們在往森林的一條遠路上奔逃著。州長的人馬朝著他們射箭，羅賓漢被射中了手。牧師迅速的爲他包紮好。羅賓漢一見到牧師的手，便將牧師的帽子掀開。

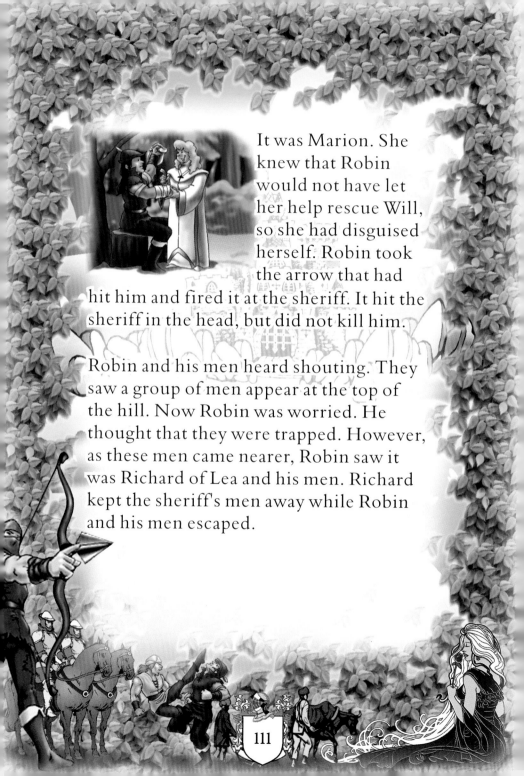

It was Marion. She knew that Robin would not have let her help rescue Will, so she had disguised herself. Robin took the arrow that had hit him and fired it at the sheriff. It hit the sheriff in the head, but did not kill him.

Robin and his men heard shouting. They saw a group of men appear at the top of the hill. Now Robin was worried. He thought that they were trapped. However, as these men came nearer, Robin saw it was Richard of Lea and his men. Richard kept the sheriff's men away while Robin and his men escaped.

牧師是瑪莉安！因爲瑪莉安知道羅賓漢將不會讓她幫忙拯救威爾，所以才僞裝自己。羅賓漢拾起射中他的箭，將它朝州長射去。箭中了州長的頭部，但是並未能致他於死地。

羅賓漢一行人聽見吆喝聲。他們看見一群人出現在山頭。羅賓漢現在不禁要憂慮了。他想他們是被困了。不過那些人更靠近時，羅賓漢發現是李縣的理察和他的人。理察將州長的人馬擋住，讓羅賓漢和其手下有時間逃離。

RICHARD OF LEA AND ROBIN HOOD CELEBRATE

The sheriff demanded that Richard of Lea opened the gates. Richard said that he wanted to see the sheriff's warrant for the arrest of Robin and his men. The sheriff became angry. He told Richard that he worked for the king. Therefore he did not need a warrant. King Richard the Lion Heart, who Richard of Lea had fought with, had returned. The evil King John was no longer king. Richard of Lea now had his lands and castle back. The sheriff could do nothing as King John was no longer king.

Richard of Lea invited Robin and his men into his castle. They had a big feast and Richard helped those who had been injured in the fight.

李理察為羅賓漢舉行慶功宴

州長命令李理察開城門。理察說他要先看州長逮捕羅賓漢和其手下的逮捕狀。州長大怒。他告訴理察他為國王工作。所以他不需要逮捕狀。李理察一向是和獅心國王理察一同作戰，現在理察國王業已歸來。邪惡的約翰國王已不再是國王了。李理察現已拿回他的土地和城堡。州長因為約翰已失去王位，也發不了威了。

李理察邀請羅賓漢和他的手下到城堡裡來。他們共享了一頓豐盛的晚餐，理察並為那些在打鬥過程中受傷的人提供幫助。

Before Robin left, Richard tried to repay Robin the four hundred pounds he had borrowed. Robin would not take the money. So, Richard gave Robin and his men new bows and arrows made of the finest wood.

Later that week, the sheriff went to see King Richard. He told King Richard about Robin Hood. He said that Robin Hood was an outlaw who killed the king's deer and did not obey the king's orders. The sheriff also said that Richard of Lea was a traitor.

在羅賓漢離去之前，理察想歸還羅賓漢借給他的四百塊。羅賓漢卻不收這錢。於是理察將上等木材製作的弓箭賜予羅賓漢和他的手下。

稍後在同一週內，州長去見理察國王。他將羅賓漢的所作所為稟告國王。他說羅賓漢是個罪犯，他捕獵國王的鹿隻，又不遵守國王的命令。州長又說李縣的理察是個叛徒。

King Richard had already heard about Robin Hood. The king decided to visit Richard of Lea and find out what had happened. Richard told the king how Robin had helped him. He explained the good deeds that Robin did. The king wanted to meet Robin Hood and asked Richard of Lea to take him to the forest.

理察國王早已聽說羅賓漢這個人。國王決定親訪李縣的理察，以了解這一切。理察告訴國王羅賓漢是如何幫助他。他解釋羅賓漢的善行。國王希望和羅賓漢見面，於是要求理察帶他到森林去。

A KNIGHT APPEARS IN SHERWOOD FOREST

After a long night of celebrations, Friar Tuck was sitting in his cottage preparing to go to bed. Suddenly there was a knock at the door. It was a knight dressed in black. The knight asked for food and a place to sleep. Friar Tuck did not want the knight to stay. However, he had no choice because the knight marched into his home and sat down. The knight was friendly to Friar Tuck and Friar Tuck felt guilty about being rude. Friar Tuck prepared food and wine and allowed the knight to sleep in his bed.

In the morning the knight said that he wanted to see Robin Hood. He had a message from King Richard. Friar Tuck pretended that he did not know Robin because he did not want Robin to be captured.

一位爵士出現在雪霧森林

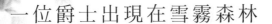

經過一整夜的慶祝，塔克修道士坐在自己的小屋裡正準備上床睡覺。突然聽見有人在敲門。門外是一名身著黑衣的爵士。這個爵士向他要食物和一個休息的地方。塔克修道士並不想讓這個爵士在家裡過夜。但他卻別無選擇，因爲那個爵士已逕自走入他的家並坐下來。爵士對塔克修道士很友善，使得修道士對自己的無禮感到抱歉。塔克修道士準備了酒菜，並讓爵士在他的床上休息。

隔天早晨爵士表示要見羅賓漢。他帶著理察國王的口信。塔克修道士裝著不知道羅賓漢這個人，因爲他不希望羅賓漢被捕。

However, he thought the knight had money, so he agreed to lead him to Robin.

As they were walking, they met Robin. Robin demanded money from the knight and said that they would prepare a feast for the knight to eat. Robin told the knight that he and his men were loyal to King Richard. He also said that they only took money from rich barons and churchmen who were usually greedy.

但是他認為爵士身上有財物，所以同意帶他去找羅賓漢。

他們在路上遇見了羅賓漢。羅賓漢向爵士索取錢財，說他們將會準備一份大餐讓爵士享用。羅賓漢告訴爵士他和他的人對理察國王都很忠心。他又說他們只向有錢的爵士和教堂的人索取錢財，因為這些人通常都很貪婪。

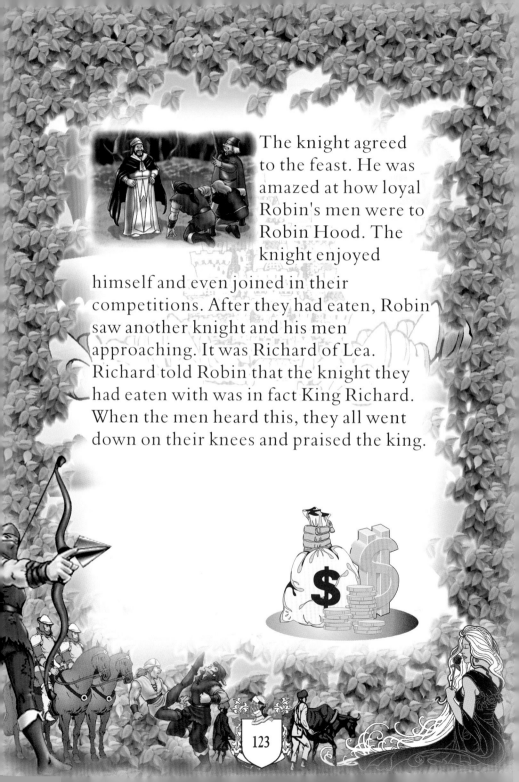

The knight agreed to the feast. He was amazed at how loyal Robin's men were to Robin Hood. The knight enjoyed himself and even joined in their competitions. After they had eaten, Robin saw another knight and his men approaching. It was Richard of Lea. Richard told Robin that the knight they had eaten with was in fact King Richard. When the men heard this, they all went down on their knees and praised the king.

爵士同意吃這一餐。他很驚訝看到羅賓漢的人對羅賓漢是如此的忠心耿耿。

爵士盡情的享用大餐，甚至還加入他們的競技。酒足飯飽之際，羅賓漢看見另一個爵士和一群人馬往這裡來。那人是李縣的理察。理察告訴羅賓漢他們宴請的這名爵士實際上就是理察國王。所有人聽到這裡紛紛下跪叩見國王。

ROBIN HOOD AND MAID MARION GET MARRIED

The king asked if Robin and his men would swear loyalty to him. Immediately all the men agreed. The king told the outlaws that they were forgiven. Their lives were no longer in danger.

However, the king told the men that they would have to live by his laws. They could not continue to live in the forest, rob people and kill the king's deer.

The king asked for Little John. Little John stepped forward and King Richard told him that he was the new Sheriff of Nottingham. The king told Will Scarlet that his father's lands, taken by the old Sheriff of Nottingham, would be given back to him.

羅賓漢和瑪莉安結為夫婦

國王問羅賓漢和他的人是否願意矢志效忠於他。所有的人立即都同意了。國王對這些罪犯說他們都被赦免了。他們將不會再有生命的危險。

然而國王告訴這些人他們必須遵守他的法令。他們將不能繼續在森林裡居住，搶劫和捕獵國王的鹿。

國王召喚短腳約翰。短腳約翰走向前去。理察國王告訴他，他將是那汀罕的新任州長。國王告訴血腥威爾，舊那汀罕州長將他父親奪去的土地將會歸還給他。

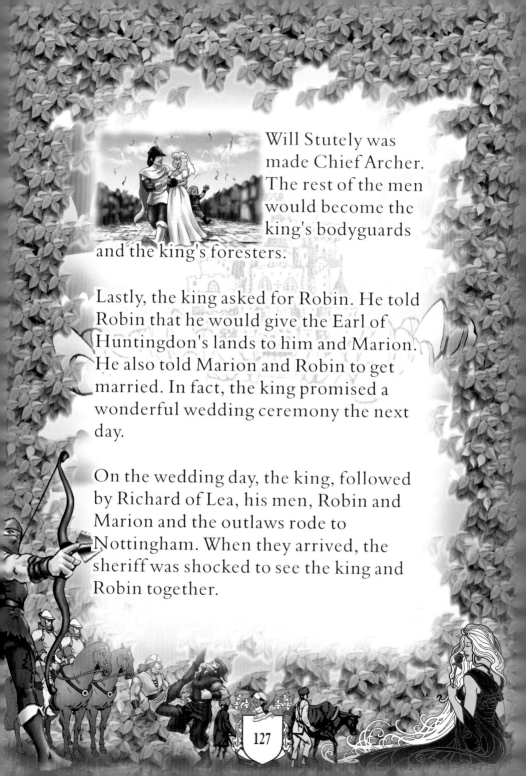

Will Stutely was made Chief Archer. The rest of the men would become the king's bodyguards and the king's foresters.

Lastly, the king asked for Robin. He told Robin that he would give the Earl of Huntingdon's lands to him and Marion. He also told Marion and Robin to get married. In fact, the king promised a wonderful wedding ceremony the next day.

On the wedding day, the king, followed by Richard of Lea, his men, Robin and Marion and the outlaws rode to Nottingham. When they arrived, the sheriff was shocked to see the king and Robin together.

威爾'史塔利被命爲第一弓箭手。其他的人則將成爲國王的護衛和狩獵人馬。

最後國王召喚羅賓漢。他告訴羅賓漢他將把杭庭頓伯爵的土地賜給他和瑪莉安。他也賜命瑪莉安和羅賓漢結婚。事實上，國王承諾在隔天爲他們舉行一個美好的婚禮。

婚禮舉行這天，國王、李理察和其手下、羅賓漢、瑪莉安及其他竊盜等一行人浩浩盪盪騎著馬到那汀罕。他們抵達時，州長看到國王和羅賓漢在一起感到非常震驚。

The king told the sheriff that he was no longer sheriff of Nottingham. He also told the Bishop of Hereford that he had to marry Robin and Marion.

The wedding was a special occasion. Young girls threw flowers on the ground as the wedding party rode to the church. Afterwards, the king arranged a feast and the celebrations continued late into the night.

國王告訴州長他不再是那汀罕的州長了。他並對曦拂主教說他必須爲羅賓漢和瑪莉安主持婚禮。

這是一場別開生面的婚禮。結婚的人馬在前往教堂的沿路上，有年輕女孩將花朵灑在地上。之後是國王安排的餐會，慶祝活動一直沿續到深夜。

HOW ROBIN HOOD MET HIS DEATH

Robin and Marion went to London with King Richard. Robin and his men who had been made the king's archers, traveled around the country settling arguments for the king over land and money. Marion became one of the finest ladies at the king's court.

However, after a few years, Robin became restless. He did not like living in a city. He wanted to go back to Sherwood Forest. He asked the king if he could travel to overseas. The king agreed and Robin and Marion traveled all over the world. However a tragedy occurred.

羅賓漢與死神交戰

羅賓漢和瑪莉安隨同理察國王走赴倫敦。被賜爲國王的弓箭手的羅賓漢和其手下在國內四處奔走，爲國王處理土地和錢財的紛爭。瑪莉安成爲宮庭內的衆美女之一。

然而數年之後，羅賓漢的心浮躁起來。他不喜歡住在城市裡。他希望回到雪霧森林。他向國王要求到海外旅行。國王允許了，於是羅賓漢和瑪莉安到世界各處去遨遊。可是悲劇發生了。

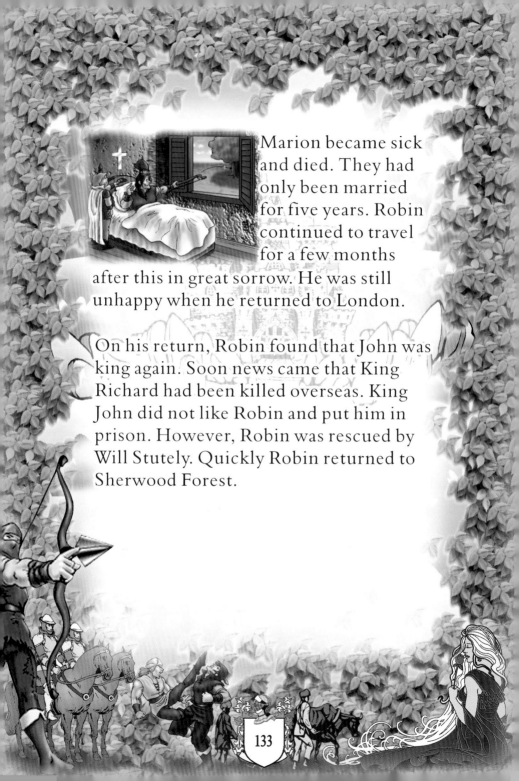

Marion became sick and died. They had only been married for five years. Robin continued to travel for a few months after this in great sorrow. He was still unhappy when he returned to London.

On his return, Robin found that John was king again. Soon news came that King Richard had been killed overseas. King John did not like Robin and put him in prison. However, Robin was rescued by Will Stutely. Quickly Robin returned to Sherwood Forest.

瑪莉安染上了病而身故。他們兩人至此結婚只有五年。之後羅賓漢帶著悲傷的心情又繼續旅行了數月。直到返回倫敦時他仍舊很不快樂。

回國之後，羅賓漢發現約翰再度成爲國王。不久消息傳來說理察國王在國外被殺。約翰國王不喜歡羅賓漢，於是將他關在監牢裡。不過威爾'史塔利將羅賓漢救了出來。羅賓漢隨即回到雪霧森林。

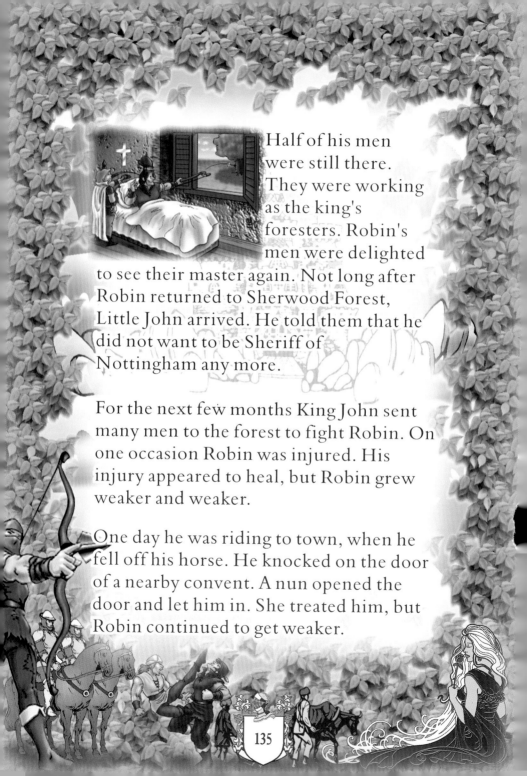

Half of his men were still there. They were working as the king's foresters. Robin's men were delighted to see their master again. Not long after Robin returned to Sherwood Forest, Little John arrived. He told them that he did not want to be Sheriff of Nottingham any more.

For the next few months King John sent many men to the forest to fight Robin. On one occasion Robin was injured. His injury appeared to heal, but Robin grew weaker and weaker.

One day he was riding to town, when he fell off his horse. He knocked on the door of a nearby convent. A nun opened the door and let him in. She treated him, but Robin continued to get weaker.

他的手下還有一半在那裡。他們是國王的狩獵人馬。他們都很高興再見到羅賓漢。羅賓漢回到雪霧森林没多久，短腳約翰也回來了。他告訴他們說他不想再當那汀罕的州長了。

接下來的幾個月，約翰國王派了許多人到森林裡和羅賓漢對抗。有一次羅賓漢負傷。雖然傷勢漸漸在復原，羅賓漢卻愈見虛弱。

有一天他騎馬進城，從馬上摔了下來。他撞到旁邊修女院的門。一名修女開了門帶他進去。雖然她爲他治療，羅賓漢仍舊愈來愈虛弱。

With his last energy, Robin blew his horn. Little John heard this and ran to the convent. He was distressed to see how ill Robin was.

For the last time, Robin picked up his bow and fired it through the window. He told Little John that wherever the arrow landed was where he wanted to be buried. The arrow hit the largest and strongest tree in the forest. Robin was buried under this tree which can still be seen today in Sherwood Forest. For many years people believed that the nun who treated Robin was in fact the old sheriff's daughter. She had finally got her revenge and killed Robin Hood.